# Madame

# Court Reporter

*by Kathy Zebert*

Kyle Roberts,

Live life in color!

Kathy Zebert

Editor: Lauren Tweedy
Cover Design: Kathy Zebert, Lauren Tweedy
Author Photo: Melody Hood, Innamorata Photography

Publisher: Words in Color Publishing
wordsincolorpublishing@gmail.com
www.kathyzebert.com

ISBN: 978-0-9967848-1-8

1. Romance 2. Legal Thrillers

Printed in the U.S.A.

The inspiration for this book comes from every single reader of the debut novel in the "Callie and Dom" series, *Incredulity*. Your love of the characters and requests for a second book were the impetus of the next chapter in my writing journey.

## Acknowledgments:

Pam Martin, Proofreader

# Table of Contents

# Madame Court Reporter

# Prologue

***San Juan, PR, November 15...***

After a six-week-long trial, Mercedes finally had the day off. It was a late night last night, with a final jury verdict at 6:30 and her second job starting at 8 p.m. and ending just after 2 a.m. She was exhausted. This was getting to be a struggle, and something was going to have to give.

Wiping the sleep from her eyes, she hit the remote to open the chic, vertical blinds covering the sliding-glass door that opened to the balcony. The sun shone in on her new red silk sheets, making them shimmer even more than she imagined they would when she bought them. She got up and slid the door open, stepping out onto the balcony. The cool breeze blew over her, sweeping her flowing, white gown against her tanned smooth skin. *What a wonderful way to start the day*, she thought.

The view over the bay from Mercedes' 21st floor condo was absolutely breathtaking today. It was one of the reasons she took the place. Sailboats were already gliding across the bay, wishing her a good morning. She could smell the coffee brewing from the kitchen, so she grabbed a cup and sat down in one of the chaise loungers on the patio.

That first taste of coffee took her mind back to the day she first arrived in Puerto Rico from Miami four years ago. She had nothing except one suitcase and a few hundred dollars, which was just enough to stay at a very dirty San Juan motel for a week. She needed a job, and she needed one quick, or she would be out on the street in a place she knew nothing about.

Determined to make a better life for herself than the one she had in Miami, she'd set out to find a job as soon as she'd laid her suitcase on the raunchy-looking, dated bedspread of her motel. It made her cringe to think about sleeping there, but it was all she could afford at the time. She'd walked up and down the streets of Miramar, asking every shop owner if they were hiring, all to no avail. She'd focused her job-seeking efforts at lavish hotels, restaurants and spas, but either they weren't hiring anyone or they weren't hiring Mercedes.

At the end of the third day, when her funds had dwindled down to forty dollars, she was beside herself with frustration and decided to sit down and relax at a local taqueria, opting for a draught beer and a taco. At one dollar total, she could really only afford one, but she hadn't eaten all day and really needed some nourishment and a fresh perspective to come up with a new plan of action.

The first bite of the crunchy taco caused the rest of the filling to fall onto her lap. *Perfect ending to a perfect day,* she'd thought. *And I've worn my last clean skirt. What's next?!* As she quickly reached for a napkin, she realized that they were so thin that it would have taken 50 of them, plus club soda, to get out that tomato and spice stain, and she couldn't afford the club soda.

Just as Mercedes was about to let out a very loud grunt in frustration, a white handkerchief had appeared in her peripheral vision, followed by a soft, masculine voice with a Hispanic accent. "Allow me to help you, young lady," said the man. "It appears you've suffered at the hands of a taco."

As Mercedes looked up, she saw an elderly man with deep brown eyes and salt-and-pepper hair smiling down at her. Her first instinct had been to decline the help with a polite thank-you, but remembering her manners, she'd simply said, "Thank you, sir. Apparently, I need an apron when eating these."

The gentleman then handed her a club soda and stood by her side while she quickly removed the stain from her skirt. He politely introduced himself as Franco Vargas and asked if he could sit. Mercedes was leery at first, but he seemed innocent enough, and she said, "Of course. Please. My name is Mercedes Cruz. It's so nice to meet you, and thank you so much for helping me. It's been quite a day."

The two began to talk, and Franco listened quietly as Mercedes detailed the previous four days and her struggle to find a job.

"As luck would have it, Ms. Cruz, you happen to be at the right place at the right time. I think I can help you find a job."

Mercedes had no idea what the offer would entail, but she was desperate for income and had been willing to do just about anything to keep herself off the streets of San Juan. Little did she know that the offer would be one that would change her life in ways she could never have imagined, comprising of a lavish but risky lifestyle.

Franco went on to explain that he was a prominent member of the judiciary in the U.S. District Court in San Juan, but he was also a Puerto Rican dignitary, of sorts. He constantly had wealthy guests visit from all over the world, and they needed to be entertained, and Mercedes would be compensated handsomely for spending time with these guests. Of course, Franco called it "spending time," but at 30 years old, Mercedes knew full well what this meant in real-world terms.

Although this was not the kind of job Mercedes had in mind when she left Miami, it was the only offer on the table, and she could make it work until she found a place to live and had enough money saved to find something better. Franco had a nice apartment on the beach where Mercedes could stay, and to ensure Mercedes' cover from any criminal prosecution, he offered her a part-time job as his court reporter.

*What?* she'd thought. *I don't know the first thing about*

*being a court reporter. How in the world will I pull that off?* But Franco assured her that she would be taken care of; he would see to it.

Of course, that was four years ago, and Mercedes had accepted the offer, and everything that came with it, with eyes wide open. The money, glamour and elegant lifestyle had consumed her in such a way that there was simply no motivation to ever leave it... until lately, when she began to tire of this man, and every other man who laid eyes on her, controlling every aspect of her life.

Finishing the first cup of coffee and opting for a second, she wasn't sure how she would regain control of the situation, but she was going to figure out a way. No man would keep her under his thumb. She'd left a life of struggles back in Miami, vowing to be in control of her own destiny.

Staring out at the beautiful, cloud-free, blue sky, Mercedes began to remember how important that was to her, and a plan began to brew in her mind. Perhaps her way out was right in front of her, within the very legal system she'd been defrauding for the last four years.

# Chapter 1: Cowboy Christmas

***Austin, TX, December 10...***

"Callie?"

"Yes?"

"Where were you just now?"

"Oh, I'm sorry, Pam. I was just thinking about Christmas at the ranch with Dom. I have no idea what to put on the menu. Do you have any ideas?"

"Well, geez, it's not as if you don't have twenty thousand recipes that you could look through. You're such an amazing cook. Whatever it is you decide, I'm sure they'll devour it," Pam replied with a cheerful smile.

"Well, thanks, my friend. I really hope so, but this has to be extra special, because we're going to have all the ranch hands and a few of Dom's business colleagues attending the party, and I want it to be perfect for Dom."

Callie hadn't planned or thrown a party in a very long time, and she was definitely remembering the stress that came with such an undertaking. The only exception to that was that Dom was taking care of the decorations and adult beverages, and she knew that was going to be perfect, because after all, he was a man who always put a plan together in a way she'd never seen anyone accomplish.

After she and Pam finished up lunch and paid the check, she gathered up her notebook and purse and drove back to the courthouse. She still had a half day's worth of plea hearings to get through before she would be able to get back to the details of the menu. Judge Goza was on the bench this week, so there was no way to get in a few minutes of anything. The bright side was that the day would go by very quickly. He certainly knew how to run a smooth docket so that everyone could get home before dark.

At the close of the docket, Callie shut down her equipment and went back to her office to get what she needed to take home. She was all caught up on transcripts for the moment, but she knew there would be a trial next week, and she wanted to research the pleadings so that her real-time would be spot on for the trial.

There would be ten attorneys, five on each side of the case, and another three or four listening in remotely; something Callie had to be ready for, both on the software and hardware end of things. Luckily, she was able to handle whatever came her way technologically, but something always failed, no matter how much prep work and testing was done prior to the trial.

As Callie pulled into the garage and worked her way through the kitchen, she turned on the coffee pot and went upstairs to change into her comfortable clothes. She came downstairs and poured her first cup of coffee, picked up her notebook and stepped out onto the patio to sit by the pool. It was a warmer-than-usual winter in Austin this year, and although the pool had to be closed, she could still sit outside comfortably with just a light sweater.

*Hmm*, she thought, *what can I put on this menu that will feed an army and that everyone will love? Oh, I know. I'll make my Cowboy Keeper Dip. It's easy to throw together in a crockpot, and everyone always stands over it at parties. One item down and tons more to go.* But as she began to think about the next item on the menu, her thoughts drifted back to the events of the last four months and how much her life had changed because of them.

What an amazing rollercoaster ride she'd been on! Before she met Dom, she thought her life was completely full, but he came blazing in like a Texas tornado and stirred up all kinds of feelings she never knew she had. She was feeling loved, for sure, and she loved him, but the relationship certainly hadn't been without doubt and turmoil.

The holidays had a way of making most of those doubts fade into the background. Perhaps they would reappear, but for now, Callie was going to enjoy what was before her at the moment. There was no point in borrowing trouble, especially not with Christmas and the new year around the corner. It was a time to be happy, and Callie was happier than she'd been in ages.

There was one thing, however, that kept creeping in and out of her conscious thoughts. In her meeting with Agent Kendrick, an opportunity had been presented. With the busy docket and all the seasonal activities, she hadn't had time to put too much effort into thinking about leaving her job and becoming an analyst with the feds. At this point, however, there was no hurry to make a decision. She would think about that after the holidays. For now, she had to get back to the party menu. It wasn't going to create itself.

One appetizer down. Maybe she should leave the main course to Dom. Beef and chicken fajitas were his specialty, and they were delicious. That was sort of the beautiful thing about planning a party together, right? And if she didn't have to think about the main course, all that was left to do were a few more appetizers, a couple of sides and, of course, desserts.

This wasn't going to be as difficult as Callie had originally thought, and the more she thought about it, the more joy filled her heart. She was really looking forward to her "Cowboy Christmas." The menu went much faster when Callie's attitude changed. It was amazing how that always worked. With bacon-wrapped pineapple and its accompanying barbecue dipping sauce, a veggie tray, and seven-layer dip, the appetizers were complete.

The sides were easy to do and always seemed to come standard with fajitas: Refried beans with pepper jack cheese and Mexican rice. And for dessert, mini black-and-blue lava cakes and white chocolate cheesecake, and perhaps a couple dozen Tuxedo strawberries, just to add a little flair.

With the menu out of the way, Callie went for another cup of coffee, put the notebook up and got out her laptop. It was time to research for the case coming up next week. When it was over, she would be off for the entire holiday season, and all of her time and attention could be focused on Dom and her family.

Looking at the clock, without realizing it, somehow 1:00 a.m. had snuck up on Callie. She quickly shut everything down and headed upstairs to bed so she could get some good sleep. It had been a productive day, but the next day was going to be tough; it was another one of those horrible child molester cases.

Even though the defendant was pleading guilty, he still had to give an allocution, and that was always torture in these cases. Every single disgusting fact of the case would be put on the record, and Callie could barely stand to be in the room during this process and spent most of the rest of the day feeling as if she needed to take a shower just to get the filth off. But it was a necessary evil in the criminal system. Someone had to make a record, and Callie knew she didn't get to pick the cases in her courtroom.

She could do it. She was a professional, after all. She just needed to remember that these were mere words. It was best to detach from the proceedings in order to avoid becoming a weeping mess on the floor. It was very similar to the mindset of a surgeon in that regard. Many of them deal with death on a regular basis, and they can't afford to get attached to the person on the table if they're going to be able to continue to be surgeons.

In her prior career, Callie worked in the medical field at a hospital. She remembered an occasion she'd walked into a roomful of anesthesiologists telling jokes about a dead man. She was only 19 at the time and found it appalling that anyone would joke about such a thing.

Watching her face, the chief anesthesiologist followed her as she left the room abruptly and explained that it was their way of dealing with a death on the table. Given her age and lack of life experience, even with the explanation, Callie didn't understand the importance of situational detachment at the time, but she certainly did now.

*Wow! That was 30 years* ago, Callie thought, as she made her way upstairs to bed. Almost as soon as her head hit the pillow, Callie was off to sleep, and the morning sun greeted her seemingly faster than that. The day came and went as she had planned, and with the words of the day behind her, it was finally Friday. A date with Dom was on the agenda. He was coming over for dinner and helping her put up the Christmas lights she'd been wanting to get up since Thanksgiving.

It had been a while since she'd made dinner for him, only because it was hard to get the jump on him when it came to giving. He always seemed to be one step ahead of her on planning things. Not that she was complaining, but every now and then, she felt as if she was getting more than she was giving, and it was nice to be able to do something special for him. She certainly didn't have the finances that he did, but she could pull her own weight and create a few little surprises for him that would make a big splash. She couldn't wait for that.

As soon as the clock struck five, it was time to shut down for the week and make a quick stop at the grocery and liquor store for a few last-minute details. Dom liked a special red with his steak, so she knew he'd be surprised that she had it waiting on the counter when he got there.

Getting home around six, she had just enough time to get the grill ready, change clothes, put on a little mood music, and throw the sweet potatoes in the oven. She was going to wear her red boots tonight. She hadn't worn them in a while, and she knew it would make Dom smile to see her in them. Plus, it came with the added bonus of making her feel special as well.

As prompt as always, Dom got there around 6:30, and as Callie opened the door and gave him a sweet kiss on the lips, she noticed he had something in his hand. She thought to herself, *of course. He never comes empty-handed.* Ordinarily, she would have been irritated, because she really enjoyed giving without receiving, but because it was Dom and relationships weren't about keeping score, she knew it was important to let him do it.

He set the purple gift bag on the bar, uncorked the wine and said, "How was your day, Darlin'?"

Callie took the glass of wine he poured for her and said, "Incomplete until just this moment," reaching in to give him a proper hello with a long, deep kiss. *This is what it's all about,* she thought to herself. She had never felt more loved and safe than when she was in his arms.

"What's in the bag, Cowboy?"

"It's a little something for my girlfriend," Dom said, giving Callie a wink.

"Lucky girl. Do I know her?"

"Not as well as I do," Dom said, "but after dinner, I thought you could take a peek and tell me if you think she'll like it."

With that, Callie took the steaks, handing Dom her glass of wine as they retreated to the patio. With the steaks on the grill, they sat down at the table, but not before Dom scooted the chairs closer together. Callie said, "So how was your day?"

"It was just a day full of horses, cows and a little talk about a business trip."

"Really?  Where to this time?  And when do you leave?"

"I have to leave just after Christmas, and I won't be back until New Year's Eve, but I'll be back that morning.  I'm not missing our first New Year's Eve together."

And there it was.  That nasty fear and doubt came rushing in.  All the business trips of the past and the lies associated with them had turned her life upside down not so long ago, but not wanting to spoil the evening and overreact, Callie simply waited for more details.

Dom must have sensed Callie's silent angst, because he said, "Don't worry, Darlin'.  I'm not involved in anything undercover, and there's nothing I'm going to hide from you from this moment forward.  You'll know everything I know as soon as I know it.  The trip is really all about the ranch in the coming year.  I'm thinking about adding another income stream to the ranch by offering a dude ranch experience, and I have meetings with other ranchers in Montana to talk about the initial planning stages."

"Oh," Callie responded.  "Sounds like an exciting project."

She tried to sound supportive and understanding about it, but there was still that nagging feeling of distrust there.  It was such an ugly feeling, but she was determined not to let it ruin the evening, so she just let it go.  If he was lying, she would figure it out sooner or later, probably sooner, but at this point, nothing good could come from creating an argument over her own trust issues.

Callie's mind quickly turned to the prospect of being involved in such an adventure. What if she was able to create some tasty menu items for the ranch guests? This could be a wonderful thing. She'd always wanted to own a bed and breakfast, and this was the cowboy version of that. The thoughts of possibilities miraculously overcame the doubt and put a smile back on Callie's face as she got up to turn the steaks, and all was well again.

An hour later, the dinner plates were in the sink. Dom went over to the bar to pour another glass of wine for the two of them and picked up the purple bag, handing it to Callie. He said, "I initially got this for my girlfriend, but since you're helping me plan the Christmas party, maybe it would be better suited for you."

"Dom, you're just about the most thoughtful person I've ever known... besides me, that is," Callie followed with a sweet little laugh.

"I hope you like it," added Dom, as Callie removed the tissue paper and reached inside the bag. She could feel something silky and thought at first it was some sexy something she could wear to bed. Instead, as she pulled the entire thing out of the bag, she couldn't believe her eyes. It was the most beautiful flouncy red dress she'd ever laid her eyes on.

Her mouth was open, but nothing would come out. She didn't know what to say, so she sat there, looking at this thing of beauty. It was clearly a designer dress, with tiny little straps, backless, with multiple layers of ruffles at the bottom, and it matched her red boots. The tag inside the bodice simply read, "Designed especially for Callie by Marrika Nakk."

"Oh, my God, Dom! How did you do this?"

"So do you like it?"

"Are you kidding me? Can you not see the look on my face? Like doesn't cover it! This must have cost you a fortune. It's way too much."

"There is no such thing, Callie, when it comes to you. I'd give everything I own to bring a smile to your face."

Tears began to well up in Callie's eyes as she jumped from her seat into Dom's lap, giving him the biggest hug she could manage with her small frame. "I can't even begin to tell you how lucky I feel to have you in my life," she whispered in Dom's ear. "You give without caution or expectation, which is not an easy thing to do at our age, given our experiences. I love the dress, but I love you more than I ever thought possible, just for being the man you are."

Dom pulled away and looked into Callie's eyes. "I'm so grateful to have found a woman who makes me feel at home in her heart."

This love was nothing like she had ever experienced. There was no waiting for the other shoe to drop. It just didn't seem as if was ever going to happen. And as they headed up to the bedroom to continue their expression of love for each other, Callie began to feel guilty about the doubts she had nearly succumbed to earlier in the evening. *Get out of your head and into your heart,* she said to herself, dismissing her guilt as she cozied up to her cowboy for the night.

Morning coffee and biscuits and gravy couldn't come soon enough the following day, and the Christmas lights were up before noon. The tree was decorated by 3:00, and after that, it was time for Callie to take a much-needed nap. Dom had work to do at the ranch, so he pulled the covers over Callie on the couch and kissed her good-bye.

"See you on Tuesday, Darlin'?"

"Hopefully, Babe," Callie whispered. She knew she couldn't depend on her day to end at a reasonable hour because of the trial the next week. It would be a very busy week. As Dom closed the door, Callie drifted off to sleep, only to be awakened 30 minutes later by a text message from her clerk, letting her know that all parties had just ordered daily copy for the trial.

Callie wasn't going to get that nap after all, at least not today. She had to get busy contacting her support staff and testing out everything before Monday. These attorneys always waited till the last minute to do everything, creating unnecessary stress for reporters.

Sunday went by much too fast, and it was time to begin the very long and stressful week. Callie had a good support team, though, and she knew that they could pull it off without a hitch. As it turned out, she was right. By the end of the week, 1500 pages had been delivered and paid for, and it was time for Callie's vacation. No more court or transcripts till the new year. It was time for a Cowboy Christmas with Dom.

The shopping experience was never something Callie looked forward to, until now. This was going to be the biggest event she'd ever planned, and she was going all out. The menu was set, and the list was made. She invited Pam along to help, with a break in the shopping action for lunch at, of course, Chuy's. Her favorite Tex-Mex restaurant for lunch seemed appropriate, given the Christmas party menu, but then again, it always seemed appropriate, especially with Pam, her favorite friend.

Shopping and lunch was a lot more fun than Callie could have anticipated, and it certainly took less time than she'd planned for. *Perfect,* she thought. *Time to spare for a glass of wine at home with Pam.* They got to Callie's house around four and put the groceries up, turned on the music and began to unwind, and Callie began her usual storytelling. It had been such a long time since the two of them had been able to just be together with no work for either of them, and work was the last thing they wanted to talk about. It was time to catch up on the things that mattered and laugh the night away.

Pam spent the night so she could drink an extra glass of wine, but got up and left for San Antonio after a quick cup of java the next morning, leaving Callie to begin the prep work for the party and spend a little quality time with Dom. The weekend flew by, and the planning suddenly became a baking frenzy for Callie.

The Christmas party was set for Friday night, and by the middle of the week, Callie had all the prep work done at her house. Dom sent over a couple of ranch hands in the SUV to transport everything out to the ranch, where she could easily finish what she hoped would be the best-tasting food she'd ever created. To facilitate that, she packed a bag so that she could stay overnight on Thursday, and possibly Friday. She knew her cowboy well enough to know that she should probably plan for a surprise or two... or three.

Dom had planned this party, and Callie had no idea what was in store for her when she set out for the ranch. As she rounded the bend to the gate, she couldn't believe her eyes. The front gate was adorned in white lights, and so was every post along the top edge of the fence on both sides of the drive up, each topped with a huge red, sparkly bow.

As she got up to the house, the two large Evergreen trees on either side of the front door were glistening in beautiful hues of royal blue and silver ornaments, and, of course, a beautiful, Texas star atop both. Callie could only imagine what the inside of the house looked like and couldn't wait to get inside. Just as she thought, Dom had the place fully decorated with cowboy Christmas decorations on the fireplace, with a pair of boots hanging from the mantle, one red and one black. She approached to get a better look, and she was thrilled to see her initial on the red one and Dom's on the black.

*Of course*, she thought to herself. Dom was nothing, if not thoughtful and detailed when it came to planning things. Looking around the room, she noticed mistletoe hanging above the archway into the dining room, which was the perfect place for it to catch someone by surprise. Just as she was about to head into another room, Dom came walking in from the patio with his usual gorgeous smile and said, "There's my sexy little cohost. Are you ready to get this party started?"

Callie reached in for a hug and a kiss and said, "I was ready yesterday. If you were waiting on me, you're way behind."

Dom laughed and said, "Always one step ahead of me, Darlin'. I knew I could depend on that. Do you have your things in the car?"

"Just a few things. I can get them later. First I want to see all these amazing decorations in a little more detail. How about a quick tour?"

"I can do that," said Dom. "I want to get your opinion on what I've done so far."

As they headed out onto the patio, Dom showed Callie the outdoor stage he'd had built for the band, but when Callie asked him who he'd scored for the band, he simply said, "Just an old friend, but I think you'll like him."

Callie had no doubt that she would and couldn't wait to see who this old friend was. This was the first time she was going to meet some of Dom's friends, and she was really excited about that.

"The pool is going to have floating lights in it," added Dom, as they passed by the area. "And the stage is set up to have a little fireworks display after the band finishes up. I thought the kids might enjoy that."

Callie replied, "And the adults too!"

Just on the other side of the stage, there was a trailer all decked out with lights and filled with bales of hay for a hayride, also for the kids. It was too warm for a sleigh, even though Dom had one of those in the stable, just in case snow appeared. Texas weather was known for its unpredictability.

"Oh my gosh, Dom!  You did such a great job with the decorations!  All we need now are people and, of course, food.  I can't tell you how excited I am to meet your friends, and for you to meet a few of mine."

Callie had invited Pam and her husband, some of her courthouse friends, and Judge Hamilton and his wife.  Ali, Cass and the precious grandbabies would be flying in from Nashville a little later, and Lauren's flight was scheduled to arrive from London in the morning.  This was going to be a blast.  She could already feel the joy in the air.

"The kids will be here tonight," said Callie, "and I want them to be able to have a place to play without worrying about them."

"Already taken care of, Darlin'.  I got a few things from the toy store yesterday and put them in the spare room in the back.  Why don't you take a look and make sure it's okay."

Callie opened the door to the spare room, and found it filled to the brim with toys.  She wasn't sure how Santa was going to be able to top Dom this year.  Callie went running back down the hallway into Dom's arms, giving him a big kiss and hug, whispering, "Thank you, my love.  Your heart is bigger than Texas."

Dom replied with a quick hug and said, "No thanks necessary, Callie.  I want them to enjoy coming here, and I want them to like me, and I'm not above a little bribery to make that happen."

*I'm in heaven*, Callie thought to herself. *I'm not sure how I got here, but I never want to leave.*

Friday would arrive before long, but for the moment, it was time to get dinner ready for the family coming into town. Dom had burgers marinating in his secret sauce, so Callie went into the kitchen to get the potatoes peeled and cut for home fries. She knew her grandkids Sophia and Michael loved those, and she loved making them for them.

In what seemed like a few minutes, the room was filled with laughter and children running from room to room... until they discovered their own little party room. Sophia came out and dragged Callie into the room to see all the wonderful surprises inside. She played with them for nearly half an hour and then left them to join Ali, Cass and Dom, who were already halfway through a beer on the deck.

Dom's son, Christopher, lived about an hour away, so he wouldn't be in until the day of the party. He had agreed to pick up Dom's mom, Nora, on his way out to the ranch. Nora and Callie had really bonded over the previous few weeks. She was such a lovely lady, and getting to know her had allowed Callie to see how Dom had become such a wonderful man.

Dinner and dessert were amazing, and with Sophia and

Michael tucked in for the night, Callie and Dom joined Ali and Cass back outside on the deck. What a perfect day this had turned out to be. It was truly one for the memory books. After one last beer, everyone decided to call it a night. The next morning would be a busy one for everyone, and Callie was fading fast from the excitement of the day.

Friday morning finally came, and Callie got up at 4:00 a.m. to get started on the desserts, since they would take the longest to finish. Dom wasn't far behind, smelling the coffee that Callie had put on to brew. He'd offered to help, but she suggested that he had plenty to do already. Dom then nodded, agreeing, but said, "Well, can I watch the master at work?"

"Of course," said Callie, "If you promise not to tell any of my secrets on how I cover up mistakes."

"All your secrets are safe with me, Darlin'."

Callie knew that was true and moved on with the preparations. Dom wasn't going to see the surprise she had in store for him, though. She was saving that for last, when he was outside or otherwise busy with his list. She knew he loved peppermint and chocolate, and she had a culinary treat for him that would knock his boots right off.

The kids were up at eight, followed by Ali and Cass, who went to retrieve Lauren from the airport. They were going to pick up breakfast on the way back for everyone, leaving Callie and

Dom to finish up the pre-party preparations. It was going to be a long, but amazing day, full of friends and family. The closer it got to party time, the more excited Callie became.

The front door flung open about an hour and a half later, and in ran Michael and Sophia, screaming with joy about, first, the doughnuts they had brought Callie for breakfast, and then all the desserts they saw on the bar in front of them. They were both just tall enough to see over the edge of the counter and reach up to grab a cookie and run off to the playroom.

Callie dropped what she was doing to give Lauren a big hug and kiss and took her coat and purse. It was time to sit for a few minutes with her children, to catch up, to smile, and just breathe the experience in. It was the first time since Mike had passed that Callie had been in a relationship, and she was thrilled that the kids seemed to like Dom and were okay with this wonderful cowboy in her life.

After an hour of relaxation, it was time to get back to work. Cass and Lauren helped Callie with the rest of the food, while Ali took Sophia and Michael out to the stables to make friends with the horses and play in the hay. The ranch was full of surprises, just waiting to be discovered by them.

Dom and the guys were busy setting tables up and putting out more decorations, setting the speakers up for the band and getting the fireworks ready for the grand show at the end of the party. Callie looked at her watch, and just as she was finishing up with Dom's surprise brownies, she said, "Oh, girls! I forgot I had to get ready. I don't think I'd make much of an impression with flour and chocolate on my face and the scent of Tabasco all over me. Time to put on my party clothes. I'll be back in a New York minute."

As was the usual course, Callie came down the hallway in a little more than half an hour. As she passed by Dom's room, the door suddenly opened, and there stood her cowboy, looking even more handsome than the night she first saw him standing beside her table on the deck of Shenanigans. He was wearing the red Polo button-down she'd bought him on one of their trips, along with a pair of black wranglers and, of course, his dress boots. There was not a single thing about this man that she would change.

Greeting her with his sweet smile, he said, "Even in my most vivid imagination, I could never have envisioned a more beautiful sight than I'm seeing at this very minute. I'm keeping you close to me all night, just in case any of my friends get any ideas about taking you from me."

"I'm all yours, Cowboy, from the tips of my toes to the top of my head. There's not a man alive who could sit in your saddle."

Apparently needing to steal a moment, Dom grabbed Callie by the hand and pulled her into the bedroom, closing the door, kissing her passionately and holding her tightly in his arms. "Just in case you needed a little reminder of where your boots are parked," Dom said as he pulled away and opened the door, taking her hand and leading her into the living room.

Callie had to take a deep breath before entering the room with the kids, and just as she did, the doorbell rang. Dom opened the door, and Callie nearly lost her balance from the face she saw on the other side. It was Willie Nelson! *What!? Shut the front door! Well, but not before letting Willie in*, Callie thought to herself. *Are you kidding me?*

Dom shook hands with Willie, and he entered the room as if he'd been there a hundred times before. And he had. This was that old friend Dom was telling Callie about, and he was right when he said she would like him. Who doesn't like Willie?

Everyone in the room was taken aback by his presence, but the guests began to arrive, and Callie didn't have an opportunity to meet him until much later in the evening, when dinner was served and people were mingling. He was just as nice as every one of Dom's friends were, which should have been no surprise to Callie. People tend to attract friends with similar personality types, and Dom was no stranger to kindness.

The party was a huge success. Pam and her husband had come for dinner, but they had to head back early to San Antonio to pick up their kids. Although a few of the courthouse staff left just after Pam, everyone else stayed to enjoy the band. The kids had a blast on the hayride. The fireworks were a spectacular display of colors as they shot up to greet the stars in the clear Austin sky. It was a perfect end to a perfect party... but it wasn't over yet.

Callie still had a surprise for Dom. She had hidden the batch of brownies she'd made especially for him, and she'd asked him to save room for his own dessert. As she brought them out and told him about them, his eyes opened almost as wide as his mouth. Callie had named them "Better Than Sex" brownies, but they were actually called Crème de Menthe brownies. And yes, they were made with Crème de Menthe. What else?

She knew Dom would devour them, and she was right. He had one bite and then took two or three in one hand, taking Callie's hand in his free hand, and headed for the patio, where a bottle of cream sherry was waiting for them.

The deck was quiet, and the mood was set, with the floating lights still aglow, making their way around the water in the pool. Cass and Ali had put Sophia and Michael down just after the fireworks and, worn out from their trip, had retreated to the upstairs wing of the house for some quality downtime. Lauren and Christopher had driven Nora home, but upon return, were upstairs in the game room, playing videogames, one of their many common interests.

This left Dom and Callie to enjoy the quietness of their own retreat by the pool. Dom said nothing until he finished the entirety of his brownies, at which point he took a drink of his sherry and said, "This has been the best Christmas I think I can remember in a lifetime of them."

"For me, too, Cowboy," agreed Callie.

"But it's not over just yet, Darlin'. I have something special for you. How about we head over to the barn for just a minute? I hid it there. And since we're going be doing our Christmases with our families separately, I wanted to give you your gift now."

Callie said, "Well, that's fine, Babe, but I didn't bring yours with me. I was planning on giving it to you on Christmas Eve."

"That's okay. You can still do that, but mine can't wait," insisted Dom.

"Well, who am I do deny my guy what he wants? Let's go. But are you sure you can move after all of those brownies you just ate?"

"Oh, don't you worry, Darlin'. It'll take more than brownies to keep this cowboy down."

Callie laughed as she got up and grabbed Dom's hand to pull him from his comfortable position in the chair, and they walked past the pool and across the way to the stables. The lights were on, and Callie could hear the horses quietly moving around in their stalls. She had no idea what was waiting for her in the stables, but she was sure it was something grand, because it would be out of character for Dom to give her anything that didn't fit that bill.

Dom went up to one of the stalls and pulled back the door, revealing the most beautiful gold mare. She had a cream-colored mane and tail and piercing blue eyes.

"Who is this beauty?" asked Callie.

"Her name is Dixie Dynamite," Dom answered," and she's your new ride."

"What?! Wow, Dom! You mean she's my Christmas present? She's just phenomenal! But this is too extravagant, Babe. I can't accept her."

"You don't have a choice, Darlin'. Number one, she's a Christmas present; and number two, she's registered in your name. You wouldn't want me to have to spend extra money to transfer her registration, now, would you?"

"Hmm... when you put it that way, I suppose not."

After a few seconds of waiting for the shock to settle in, Callie suddenly realized she'd heard something familiar about the mare's name. Wanting to confirm what she thought she'd heard, she asked, "Wait a minute. What did you say her name was?"

"Dixie Dynamite. It sort of reminded me of you, but if you don't like it, we can change it."

"Oh, my God! You have no idea how perfect that name is

as a gift for me, Dom."

"Really?  Do tell?"

Callie then began to tell Dom a wonderful memory from her past, where her dad had bought her a CB radio as a bribe to skip her junior year in high school.  He wanted her to finish early and move on to college, but Callie needed a little persuasion because she was going to have to give up six weeks of her summer. He'd asked what would do the trick, and Callie's request was a CB. She'd given herself the handle of Dixie Dynamite.

"It must be fate," Dom said at the end of Callie's sweet story.

"Undoubtedly, a gift in more ways than one.  I love her, and I love you for always wanting to put a smile on my face.  You know that you don't have to shower me with all of the lavish gifts, though, right?"

"It's not about 'have to,' Darlin'.  It's about 'get to,'" Dom whispered, leaning in to give Callie another one of his sweet kisses.  Callie spent the next half hour getting to know DD, as she lovingly decided to call her.  She brushed her coat, patting and rubbing her, talking to her softly.  Callie knew that they were going to be the best of friends in no time at all.

As they put DD down for the night, Dom and Callie walked arm-in-arm back to the house and into the bedroom, where Callie could give Dom a proper thank-you for DD, and Dom could remind her why the name of those brownies should be changed back to Crème de Menthe. It had been an astounding couple of days, and Callie wasn't sure she could sleep, but she drifted off in Dom's arms, as usual.

The following morning, Callie heard Sophia and Michael and got up to turn on cartoons and make breakfast. After breakfast, Ali, Cass & Lauren packed up and got ready to go to Callie's, where they would spend the next week. Sophia and Michael took a little coaxing to get out of the playroom, but Dom promised that the next time they came out, he'd take them out to the lake and let them fish. That did the trick, and they quickly stepped up into their car seats and were ready to go.

Callie kissed Dom and thanked him for the wonderful party. They agreed to meet on Christmas Eve morning so that she could give him his gift. On the drive home, Lauren and Callie had some quality mother-daughter time, talking about Lauren's writing assignment in London over the past few weeks. With Callie's free time over the next week, they would do some shopping and baking and enjoying being together as a family, which was a rarity as of late.

Family time was just what Callie needed. Although she had been plenty busy with Dom, work and her friends, she had really missed her children. They both had become busy with their own lives, as kids do, and it was good to finally just be together for several days in a row so that everyone could recharge their batteries.

Thursday, Christmas Eve, finally came, and Callie couldn't wait for Dom to walk in the front door for lunch. He must have been excited about it as well, because he got here two hours early. The kids had run out for a few last-minute items, so Callie and Dom had some time alone. Callie reached under the tree and presented Dom with a black satiny envelope, which he carefully opened.

"Just rip it open, Silly," suggested Callie.

"No, ma'am. I'm not going to ruin this envelope. This one's a keeper," Dom followed quickly.

Once opened, he pulled out the contents and opened a card with a weekend hotel reservation confirmation and a printed certificate that said, "Welcome to the BMW Driving School." This was a whole other sort of race, and Dom immediately began to smile.

"Are you serious? How did you know I've been wanting to get my baby on the track in Greenville?"

Callie was overjoyed and replied, "Oh, good! You like it, then?"

"What's not to like? Zooming around the track in my Beamer with you by my side? That's a fantasy."

"I'm so glad you like it, but it's really for you and

Christopher. I've noticed a little tension between the two of you, and I thought you could use some bonding time."

Looking at Callie with the saddest face she'd ever seen, Dom said, "You are very intuitive, Callie. We've been struggling for a while. I'm not sure how to communicate with him. He's nothing like me, and I don't know how to get through."

"He's much like you, Babe. You just don't see it because he's not a working cowboy. He has your kind heart, your gorgeous smile, and your beautiful brain. He's just trying to make his own mark in the world, the same as you when you were his age. Am I right? Would you be at the ranch if your dad hadn't died?"

"Again, right on the mark, Darlin'. Maybe we do need some guy time to have a better understanding and reconnect, man to man. This was such a thoughtful gift, Callie. I think I'll keep you around a little while longer," Dom said, as he gave Callie a wink, followed by a sensuous kiss and a warm hug.

"That's a good thing, because I'd hate to have to find a place for DD to stay," Callie responded with a reciprocal wink.

With that, the kids came bolting in the door with their arms full, and Callie and Dom got up to help. Lunch was over in a heartbeat, and it was time for Dom to say good-bye for a week. Callie walked him out to the truck for a hug, neither of them wanting to let go.

"See ya' on New Year's Eve, Darlin'," Dom said.

"Can't wait, Cowboy," Callie said, blowing Dom a kiss as he pulled out of the driveway.  It was going to be a long week.

## Chapter 2: Turning the Tides

***San Juan, PR, December 27...***

Mercedes had been hoping to see her family in Miami for the holidays, but it didn't appear to be in the cards. Christmas had come and gone, and she was desperately missing her family. Although she had no court cases on her docket until the beginning of the new year, Franco had set up several parties for her to attend over the holidays and refused to allow her to leave.

It had become all too apparent to her that he was holding all the cards, and she was no longer in control of what was happening in her life, either inside or outside of the courtroom. She'd been trying to think of a way to turn things in her favor, but hadn't come up with a plan as of yet. There had to be a way out, and her desire to get out of this quagmire without going to prison was increasingly present in her mind. She'd left Miami to free herself from one difficult set of circumstances, and she now found herself in an even worse situation. The straightjacket was coming off; it was only a matter of how.

The morning newspaper had just hit the front door, and Mercedes decided to take in the view on the balcony with a fresh cup of eye-opening java. She normally skipped the front-page articles because they were mostly about corruption and politics, and she already knew as much as she wanted to about those topics. Just as she was about to flip to the sports section, however, a big, bold title of an article on the front page caught her eye. "Whistleblower Outs U.S. Customs."

Mercedes began to read the article about how an anonymous whistleblower uncovered a ring of Customs officers confiscating items in packages and selling them in the black market. Could something like this be the answer to her dilemma? She immediately put the newspaper down and decided to get her laptop from the kitchen table and look up the whistleblower statute. Even though she knew nothing about the law previously, her "pretend" job had been educating her since her time in it. *This could prove to be really beneficial*, she thought to herself.

As she reviewed the statute and all the information about it, she wasn't sure her anonymity would be protected, in light of the fact that the courts were the ones who were in charge of reviewing things. Franco had too many friends in high places. Just as she was about to give up on the notion of help from the government, she remembered that she had a friend back in the States who worked for the Department of Justice. Perhaps whistleblowing wasn't the way to go, but her contact at the DOJ may know of something else.

Mercedes decided it was time to share her story with someone else, and she knew that she could trust this particular friend because they came from a similar background and had shared secrets before. They'd even had a code word set up, just in case either of them was ever in trouble and needed help. She hoped her friend, Sabrina, would remember, because the word "troublemaker" had been decided on when they were in their teens, and thankfully, neither of them had ever had to use it.

But what if Franco had her phone tapped? One of the perks of being an insider in Franco's corrupt little scheme is that she had been instructed to use burner phones for that business. There were plenty of them stashed in Mercedes' wall safe behind her dresser. *Perfect use of the tools of the trade to take him down*, Mercedes thought. She simply reached into the safe for a brand-new one and made the call.

As soon as Mercedes pressed "send" on the call to Sabrina, she began to question what she was doing. The proverbial cat would be out of the bag once she made this phone call, and there would be no turning back, and she had no way of knowing what was on the other side of this decision. Sabrina picked up on the first ring, however, and when Mercedes heard her soft voice saying, "Hello?" she simply responded with, "Hello, troublemaker."

Apparently remembering the code word, Sabrina responded, "Let me call you right back on my other phone," and hung up. A few seconds later, Mercedes' phone began to ring, but the info on the call registered as 000-000-0000.

"Hello?" Mercedes said, pausing a second or two.

"What's wrong, Mercedes?" asked Sabrina.

Mercedes began to cry, but through the tears and moments of sobbing, began to recount every word of the whole ugly story that had become her life in San Juan. Sabrina sat silent, listening until the end, at which point she said, "My lovely girl, I know someone who can help. You're not alone. I'm going to help you get to the other side of this. It's not going to be easy, but it will be worth it. So stop your crying. You did the right thing by coming to me. Don't say anything to anyone. I'm going to hang up and get the wheels in motion on this and get back to you ASAP."

Mercedes responded, "Thank you, Sister. I knew I could count on you. I'll do as you ask and wait to hear from you."

"Of course you can. Always," Sabrina said, and then hung up.

Looking through teary eyes out into the blue-green water across the bay, Mercedes felt better for the first time in many months. The uncertainty of her future at this point was certainly far better than the certainty of her present. This was the way she felt when she'd left Miami, but she was hopeful that the next chapter in her life would bring with it the opportunity of a respectable lifestyle, if such a thing existed for her.

Given the nature of both of her current professions, Mercedes had become the queen of pretending. She was not emotionally attached to anything or anyone, pretty much the entire time she was awake. Now that a plan was in place and the window was beginning to open, allowing her to breathe a little easier, pretending would be a breeze. She was finally feeling a slight sense of relief and decided to take a morning walk along the beach. Sand between her toes and the smell of the ocean would be a peaceful getaway from all the stress.

The following day, there was a buzz on Mercedes' intercom. She pressed the button, and said, "Yes?" It was the FedEx man. She buzzed him up, and within a few minutes, he was knocking on the door. She opened the door, signed on the computer screen, thanked him while taking the package, and closed the door.

Inside the package was a phone, with a note from Sabrina instructing Mercedes that she should use this phone for all communications with her from this point forward; that it was a secure line. "Agent Frank Kendrick will be in touch with you on this phone tomorrow at 2 p.m. You can trust him. He's a personal friend of mine. He will take care of you, Doll."

Exactly at 2 p.m. the following day, Agent Kendrick called and made an offer Mercedes couldn't turn down. He was going to give her immunity from prosecution in exchange for her testimony against the entire criminal enterprise. But there would need to be evidence gathered before that could happen, which could put her life in jeopardy. When Mercedes expressed her concerns about that, Agent Kendrick told her that he would be sending someone to help her gather evidence, adding that it would be best if she didn't know the details. This man clearly didn't know anything about her, because she was a woman who needed to know everything that affected her life.

Mercedes took a deep breath and slowly exhaled as she hung up the phone and laid it on the coffee table. The room was quiet except for the very loud and irritating second-hand ticking of the antique Gilbert clock sitting on the fireplace mantel. She really hated not knowing the details about what she'd set in place. For now, though, her need to control would have to be relinquished to a higher power, and she had to have faith that she'd made the best decision for herself and her future.

On the heels of that very thought, she took another deep breath, this time taking a sip of her now-tepid coffee and raising the cup towards the ceiling. "Here's to you, Mommy. I know you're watching over me."

Now steadfast in her plan of action, Mercedes felt a sense of peace. As she closed her eyes and took another relaxing breath, she had a vision of a kind, beautiful woman walking out of the darkness and into the room. Startled, she quickly opened her eyes to an empty room. Dismissing the vision as a memory of her mom who had died when she was six, she began to get ready for what she hoped would be one of her last requisite dates.

### *Austin, TX, December 29...*

The time between Christmas and New Year's seemed to be moving at a snail's pace, for some reason. Callie hadn't heard a word from Dom the entire time he'd been gone, and she missed him terribly. She knew he was in some pretty intense business meetings, though, and he'd be home soon enough.

Even though she wasn't normally the type of woman who was insecure, or really even concerned, when a man didn't call, she was annoyed that she was even feeling slightly anxious about it. She knew that those nagging doubts were to blame, but she wasn't going to let them ruin her day and decided to take a run and leave the doubts in the dust behind her.

The three-mile run through the back side of the neighborhood felt good to Callie's body. The holidays had caused a few extra pounds to find their way into her ordinarily flat belly, and with the kids visiting, she hadn't been able to get in her usual exercise regimen. No matter what the exercise had been throughout all of Callie's adult life, she'd found it to refresh her body and rejuvenate her mind. Today, it seemed she needed it more than she had in a while.

On Callie's way in the front door, she took a brief look at her cell phone lying in the basket on the entryway table to check for messages. There was a message, but from an unknown number. She felt excited just thinking about the possibility that Dom had called from a phone other than his cell and immediately pressed the button to listen to the voicemail.

"Ms. Fletcher, I hope you had a nice holiday. This is Agent Frank Kendrick. I have an urgent matter to discuss with you. Would you give me a call as soon as possible, please? My private line is (212) 420-0001."

*Hmm*, Callie thought. *I told him I'd think about his offer and get back to him. Is he going to put pressure on me? I haven't made a decision yet.* Callie hated high-pressure tactics. What did he want that was so important that she had to call immediately? Of course, she knew speculation was only for people who didn't need to know an answer or couldn't possibly find the answer, and that wasn't the case here. She could find the answer to her question by calling.

Opting to shower and change clothes first, she put her phone back down on the table and went upstairs to wash the dust and sweat off her body. A half an hour later, invigorated from the run and the shower, Callie came downstairs to return Kendrick's phone call. She already knew the answer she was going to give if he asked her again about her decision. She hadn't decided yet, and that was that.

Unfortunately, the phone call wasn't about that offer at all, and the conversation that followed nearly caused Callie to drop the phone. There was no way she could have prepared an answer for this request.

"Hi, Agent Kendrick. This is Callie Fletcher, returning your call."

"Yes, Callie. Thank you for getting back to me so quickly. I've had a situation arise that I need your help with. I know that we left things in a holding pattern at our last meeting, and you were going to get back to me; however, this is an entirely different and urgent matter, and I can't wait for an answer."

"Really? What's going on?" Callie asked in a reluctant but genuinely curious tone.

Kendrick replied, "I have an undercover assignment that's right up your alley..."

Callie took the phone away from her ear and shook it a couple of times, walking out to the patio. Did she have a bad connection? What did he just say?!

"I'm sorry, Agent Kendrick. Can you repeat what you just said? I don't think I caught it."

"Sure. I know it sounds a little crazy, but I have an undercover assignment that I need your help with," Kendrick restated.

"Have you lost your mind?" Callie said, in a little bit of an unprofessional tone, simultaneously shaking her head from side to side. "I'm not qualified for undercover work. Why on Earth would you even consider asking me to do something like that?"

Realizing her tone and remembering she wasn't talking to Pam or one of her children, Callie quickly apologized.

Accepting her apology, but continuing on, Agent Kendrick said, "Give me a second to explain, Callie, and I think you'll understand."

"Uh, okay," Callie agreed, thinking she was going to need something a little stronger than tea for this conversation.

"I've become aware of an allegation of a continuing criminal enterprise involving a young woman in Puerto Rico. She says that she's been working as an official court reporter for a federal judge, but that she's doing so only as a cover for her participation in a well-organized escort service run by the judge, who's also a Puerto Rican dignitary. The young woman wants out and is willing to testify against the judge and his coconspirators, but we need more. That's where you come in."

Callie interrupted again, asking, "How is it I factor into this situation?"

"We need evidence, not only about the reported criminal activity, but also of the credibility of this young woman. What she's reporting is, as you well know, a very serious accusation against a powerful person; and if it's true, it's one of the worst forms of governmental corruption I've ever seen."

Callie was still listening intently, but her question still hadn't been answered. So she asked again, "I still don't understand. How is it that you think I can help you with this case?"

Kendrick simply responded, "Because of your experience as a court reporter, as a highly ethical professional who honors the judicial system, and because of your amazing ability to analyze and uncover the tiniest of details. You have what it takes to become a spy. I've done this long enough to know those qualities when I see them."

For the first time in Callie's life, she had no words. She was trying to form a few congruent thoughts so that she could ask more questions, but her lips couldn't even close at this point. Several seconds passed, and then the boiling water made itself known with a very loud whistle, giving Callie a way to escape the awkward silence... and the conversation.

"Callie?" Kendrick said, wondering if she was still there.

"Yes, I'm here," Callie responded. "Give me just a minute to pour a cup of tea and gather my thoughts. You just said a mouthful there. I'm going to put the phone down, but I'll be right back."

Taking the time to pour the water, put the bag in and leave her tea to steep for a few minutes, Callie returned to her call. She could finally ask a coherent question or two, the first of which was, "What exactly do you want me to do?"

Agent Kendrick answered, "What you do best, Callie. Discover the truth. As for the details, I need you to be on a flight to DC on January 2. I know this is sudden, but the clock is ticking on this one, and you'll need to be put through an intense CIA training program. I want you armed with all the intellectual and physical tools necessary to protect yourself as an undercover operative."

The tea wasn't going to help Callie in this particular situation. She was yet again unable to form a single thought, and the details were coming at her like speeding bullets from an AK-47. Feeling the need to drop the phone and run to the bathroom to relieve the queasy feeling in the pit of her stomach, she said, "I'm going to need to think about this and get back to you."

"I understand, Callie, but I'm going to need an answer by the end of the day. You can text me your answer, and I'll make all the arrangements and send you the details tomorrow."

"Wow. A moment's notice to shake up your entire life?" Callie said with a sense of disbelief. "But what about my job? I can't just leave."

"As I said," Kendrick replied, "I'll take care of the details. You just have to give me your answer by the end of the evening."

Agreeing to his request, Callie hung up the phone and swapped out her tea for three fingers of vodka. *What just happened?"* she thought. *There's just no way I can do this.* But as the details of the conversation sank in a little deeper, Callie began to think about the young woman in Puerto Rico. What if this were true? How could she say no? But then again, how could she say yes? There were too many unanswered questions and no time to think all of this through in her normal reasoned fashion.

After about 15 minutes, the effects of the vodka kicked in and slowed Callie's mind and pulse to a point that she could make a decision without overthinking it. Perhaps it wasn't a decision that should have been made with the help of alcohol, but Callie knew that she'd never agree to this sort of risky venture stone-cold sober. Besides, at the end of the day, if it all went south, she could blame the vodka. Nevertheless, she knew what she had to do. She was in.

Callie made the phone call to Agent Kendrick, confirming her acceptance of the assignment, after she gave her body enough time to get rid of the extra help from the vodka, followed by that trip to the bathroom she had needed before the vodka. Dom would understand. And if he didn't, he wasn't the man she believed him to be.

The next few days were full of anticipation and sketchy details. Callie received a FedEx envelope from Kendrick the day after her phone call with him, but all she really knew was that she had a flight on a private jet to DC at 9:00 a.m. on January 2, where she would be greeted by Agent Kendrick and his assistant. Kendrick had arranged for a 30-day leave of absence from her job in Austin, under the guise of an out-of-state emergent family medical situation.

Now knowing that she could be away for up to 30 days, the hard reality of Callie's decision to commit to this assignment came crashing in like a rogue wave in a tropical storm. The instinct to renege immediately kicked into high gear, but she knew that instinct was simply the product of fear, and it would pass; at least, she hoped it would. *A tiny bit of fear is a good thing to keep in my pocket*, she thought to herself. *It keeps my senses on high alert.*

When she was deep in thought about the enormity of the events to come, Callie's phone rang, startling her to the point of knocking her nearby bottled water to the floor. Her pulse seemed to race with it as it rolled across the ceramic tiles, finally stopping under one of the kitchen cabinets. Her eyes finally turned from the bottled water back to her phone, and she realized it was Dom calling.

She quickly answered to hear his deep, raspy voice say, "Hey, Darlin'. My flight just landed, and I can't wait to see you. Are you busy, or can I head that way now?"

Smiling from ear to ear, Callie responded in a way that Dom would be sure to hear the excitement in her voice. "Don't stop anywhere in between!  I need to smother you with all the hugs and kisses I've been saving up for a week."

"Well, I'll break a few traffic rules for that," Dom replied, laughing.

"And I'll pay for every ticket you might get along the way," Callie said.  "Hurry up, Cowboy!  My lips and arms are getting lonelier by the second."

As soon as she hung up the phone, all thoughts of anything except Dom went right out the open patio door and off into the beautiful Austin skies.  She was so happy that he was on his way, and she went upstairs to put on the sexiest lingerie she could find so that she could let him know just how much she'd missed him.

Hearing Dom's truck pulling into the driveway, Callie went to the bar to pour a scotch for him.  She knew he'd be tired and a little jetlagged from his flight.  It was nearly 4:00, and she wasn't going to let him go back to the ranch tonight.  She had plans for a loving and relaxing evening in store for him.

Dom knocked on the front door, and she greeted him, wearing her short, red, silky robe, handing him the scotch. "Welcome home, Babe," Callie said, embracing him tightly.

One look was all it took for Dom to quickly close the front door, put the drink on the entry table and disrobe Callie, as he said, "I don't want any of my senses dulled for this." He took her by the hand and walked with her to the sofa, and their own personal nonalcoholic happy hour began.

Lying there in the afterglow of their lovemaking, Callie could hear Dom's breaths against her face. They were slow and deep, indicating the familiar state of sleep. She closed her arms even tighter around him and snuggled her head into the nape of his neck, falling peacefully asleep beside him.

Two hours later, Dom began to stir, and Callie could feel the warmth of his gentle kiss on her forehead. She opened her eyes and looked up at him with a smile. Although she didn't want to move, she was getting hungry, and she knew he must be starving because he'd come straight there and more than likely had only eaten snack food on the flight home.

"Are you hungry, Cowboy?" Callie asked.

"That would be an understatement, but I really don't want to move from this spot."

"Do you think the spell will break if we do?"

"There's not a chance of that happening, ever, but maybe just a few more minutes of holding you in my arms while we think about what we're hungry for."

They both agreed to pizza delivery from the shop around the corner, which would give them 45 more minutes to enjoy just being still in each other's arms, catching up on the week. Callie was listening intently to Dom as he highlighted his meetings in Wyoming. He came back with some inspiring ideas for the dude ranch, and she watched as his gorgeous blue eyes lit up when he spoke about the potential income it could bring to the business. It wasn't just the money, he explained. This was right up his alley. He was a cowboy at heart, and a dude ranch would allow him to immerse himself in all that the cowboy lifestyle stood for; from teaching riding and roping lessons, to sharing with others his love of the outdoors, horses and entertainment.

Without realizing it, half an hour had wound around on the clock, and the doorbell rang. The pizza was early, for a change. Callie grabbed her robe and ran into the guest bathroom as Dom pulled on his jeans and T-shirt and exchanged a fifty-dollar bill for pizza held by a young delivery guy, who reached for change.

"Keep the change, my man," Dom said with a grin.

"Really? This is a fifty?! The pizza is twenty dollars, sir."

"Is that not enough of a tip?" Dom said in a joking tone.

"Sir, that's the biggest tip I've ever gotten! I just wanted to be sure you knew you'd handed me that large a bill."

"You just kept me from having to leave my lady for even a second, which is worth every single penny. If you could do that for me every day, you'd be a rich man. Keep up the good work, son."

"Wow! Then I wish I could work for you, sir. Thank you so much!"

"Save it for a rainy day. You might need to tip somebody for your own special lady one day," Dom said, closing the door.

White cheddar and sausage pizza never tasted better than it did that night. Callie and Dom ate an entire pizza and continued to talk for the next few hours. Although Dom had asked Callie how her week had gone, she'd declined to mention anything about the "Puerto Rico Project." It just wasn't the right time, and she wasn't sure how to broach the topic with him. She decided that sleeping on it would be a better alternative.

After dinner, the two returned to their previous comfortable positions on the down-filled sofa and snuggled in to watch a quiet movie, simply enjoying being together. Callie whispered to Dom, "I missed you, Babe," but as she heard no response, she looked up to find him already dozing, with a sweet, boyish smile on his lips. She couldn't help but wonder if that smile would remain the following day, when she'd have to talk to him about her new assignment. *Relax,* she thought. *Tomorrow may not come, and that smile is all that matters tonight.*

But tomorrow did come, and Callie woke up to the sound of Dom's attempting to quietly make coffee and breakfast in the kitchen. It was sweet that he tried, but she'd been a light sleeper since becoming a mom, and her senses were further heightened now that she lived alone.

"What's cookin', Cowboy?" Callie asked, without opening

her eyes.

"Oh, I thought I might make my mama's biscuits and gravy. Are you okay with that, or do you want to go out for breakfast?

"You're kidding, right?" Callie quickly responded, getting up and walking into the kitchen. "I haven't seen you in a week, and I'm not ready to share you with the world for a while. We could have toast for breakfast, and it wouldn't matter as long as you're here with me. The biscuits and gravy are simply an amazing bonus."

"Well, you're in luck, Darlin', because the next 24 hours are all about us. No outsiders allowed until next year. I have a surprise planned out at the ranch for you. I want to celebrate our first New Year's Eve together in style. What do you say we head out after breakfast and take DD for a ride? We can pack a picnic and make a day of it. It's beautiful weather outside."

"I love that idea almost as much as I love you, Dom! I can't wait to get to know my sweet DD!" Callie said, hugging Dom from behind and giving him a kiss on his shoulder.

After breakfast, Callie threw a few things in her bag, and the two left for the ranch. When they got there, Dom got the picnic basket, threw in food and beverages for the day, and they both walked over to the stables to get the horses ready. Callie hadn't seen DD since before Christmas, and Dom thought it would be a good idea to spend a little time with her before she attempted to saddle and mount.

"Hey, sweet girl," Callie said, as Dom opened DD's stall door. "Remember me? You're such a beauty! I really missed you." Callie began to softly rub DD's mane and pat her side as Dom showed her how to tack DD up. Callie knew nothing about tacking, and watching Dom's gentleness and experience in getting DD ready to ride was mesmerizing. Callie was in love with a true cowboy; something she'd never envisioned would happen in her life. She felt as if she was in one of those movies she loved to watch with her daddy, and it filled her to the brim with joy.

DD was ready to ride, but Callie took the bridle first and walked with her over to the stall where Dom's favorite ride, Yin Yang, was waiting. He was clearly excited when he heard Dom and Callie getting closer. Callie could hear his anxious whinnying and smiled at Dom. DD apparently wasn't amused, as she shook her head back and forth.

Dom quickly got Yin Yang saddled up, helped Callie mount DD, hopping into his own saddle like the pro that he was, and they began their show walk out of the stable and into the pasture. Callie had no idea where they were going, but it didn't matter. She was with this amazing man, riding on this gorgeous mare, and life couldn't be better.

A few miles into the pasture, Dom looked at Callie and

asked, "Are you ready to pick up the pace a little?"

"Uh, I'm not sure."

"If you're not comfortable, we can walk for a bit more, but I want to give my buddy a little extra exercise today, and DD could use some too. We're not going to run hard, just trot speed. Baby steps, Darlin'. She's going to take care of you, and so will I. Do you trust me?"

"With my heart, my mind, and my body," said Callie.

"That's my girl. Then give her a little kick on both sides and let her know you're ready."

And with that, Callie and Dom trotted just until the clearing ended, and Dom told Callie to pull up on the reins slowly, letting DD know it was time to slow down again. Maneuvering through trees and little rough terrain, Callie was beginning to get comfortable with DD; and DD with her. The winding, hilly trail was full of towering magnolia trees; something Callie didn't expect to see on a ranch. Dom mentioned that his dad had purposely kept them when clearing this part of the ranch.

They were a welcome sight for Callie, who had one in the front yard of her Mississippi childhood. Nearly every special occasion was memorialized by a photo of Callie in front of that tree. Prom, that tree; Easter, again, that tree. New car, yes, that tree. It seemed the day was going to be comprised of numerous reasons to smile.

At the top of what felt to Callie like the fiftieth hill, the terrain finally evened out, and she could hear the sound of flowing water. Dom, who had been following her from behind, trotted up beside her and asked, "Are you ready for that picnic? It's almost noon, and the horses could use a drink and a snack."

"I'm starving, and a little saddle sore," said Callie. "I'd love to take a break and stretch."

"Great! There's a place up here where we can lay everything out and rest for a while."

Several hundred yards through pine and ash trees and around a short bend, a magical place appeared in Callie's view. It was a natural waterfall, flowing freely from about 50 feet above, over the jagged edges of limestone and down into a small pond that fed the creek bed downstream. Around one side of the pond was a grassy area, the perfect place to picnic. *Was this what heaven looked like?* Callie wondered. *It's as close as I'll get on this side of the fence.*

Callie and Dom dismounted as they got to the creek, leading the horses to the edge to drink and graze, and Dom spread out a couple of thick blankets on the grass as Callie got out their lunch from the picnic basket. Lunch in front of a waterfall with this gorgeous man by her side was a fantasy Callie could never have dreamed, even in her wildest imagination. She found herself wishing that every woman could feel this way.

Callie wanted time to stand still. There was something about being in this place that made that seem possible. She wanted to make this memory last with all of her senses. Closing her eyes for a few seconds, she could hear the trickling of the water as it said a quick "hello" to the pond below. The cool breeze whisked her blonde locks, brushing them against her brow. She breathed in the scent of Dom's cologne mixed with the scents of his beautiful body.

She found herself drifting back to her teenage years, fishing alongside her brother in the backyard of a family friend who lived on the Ross Barnett Reservoir. They'd been there for hours and caught nothing. He was the only guy she'd ever enjoyed fishing with, because he didn't mind baiting her line and taking off the fish she caught. Callie only enjoyed the thrill of hooking and reeling the fish in. The rest was gross.

Back on that smoldering August Mississippi day, they'd been throwing out lines all day, and nothing was biting except the turtles. Criss had put the last of the bait on Callie's hook and said, "Throw it out one more time, and then let's go." The line was cast, and a few seconds later, Callie felt a tug, and the bobber dropped beneath the water.

Criss was packing up the tackle box, and Callie said, "I think I've got something." Criss said, "It's probably another turtle," looking out to the water. But as one tug turned into multiple tugs, nearly pulling the pole from Callie's grasp, Criss began to get wide-eyed and excitedly instructed her on the proper reeling procedure.

Struggling, but determined not to be defeated by her unknown aquatic competitor, she reeled in the biggest catfish she would ever catch. As she looked at her brother, the excitement in his eyes told her everything she needed to know about what kind of man he would become. He was more excited that she'd caught this fish than he would have been if he'd caught it himself.

They took the fish home, and Criss got out their dad's Polaroid camera. Pride in Callie taking over his senses, he used the entire pack of film on Callie and the fish. Then he showed Callie how to clean it, and she remembered not even being bothered by the splatter of fish blood onto her favorite T-shirt.

Although there were no scales to weigh the fish, it was big enough for the two of them to eat for dinner. So Callie fried it up with a cornmeal batter, joined by its friends, fried potatoes and hushpuppies. It had been a day to remember, one that would last as long as she lived.

"Callie," Dom interrupted. "Are you okay?"

"No. 'Okay' doesn't describe what I'm feeling," she said, giving Dom a full smile. "And I'm not sure I can define the feeling, because putting words to it seems to limit it somehow. Let's just say I'm feeling extremely blessed. That should cover it. Thank you, Babe, for this day, and for every day since we met."

"There are many more days like this, Darlin'. The best is still waiting for us on the other side of tomorrow."

And as those words passed through his lips and into Callie's ears, reality came crashing in. It was time. She had to talk to him, and although she detested conflict of any sort, she needed to tell him about her upcoming undercover assignment. As her grandma used to tell her, she'd have to put on her big-girl britches and deal with it.

Callie began to struggle with the words to begin the conversation, and Dom seemed to notice. "Something on your mind, Callie?"

"How do you always seem to know that? Am I that transparent?" Callie asked.

"Only when you're quiet," Dom answered as he gave Callie a wink. "What's on that beautiful mind?"

"Do you remember the meeting I had with Frank, where he offered me the analyst job with the feds?"

"Sure. You were going to think about that and let him know. You haven't talked about it lately. Have you been giving it more consideration?"

"Well, yes and no," Callie said, and began to give Dom the details of the Puerto Rico special assignment.

Dom was completely silent through the entirety of Callie's

recounting of what transpired while he was out of town. She watched his bright blue eyes to see if she could get a read on his feelings, but he was obviously very good at keeping things under wraps because of his own history in the undercover business.

As soon as the details were out, Callie took a deep breath and said, "So I have to leave the day after tomorrow." Dom was taking way too long to respond, but Callie still had no idea what he was thinking. Of course, she'd already made the decision, but she wanted Dom's seal of approval, or at least some sort of understanding. Going away for a month after an unresolved disagreement with her beautiful cowboy wasn't something she was relishing.

After a really long few minutes, Dom finally began to share his concerns and ask her for more details. Callie didn't realize how little she knew about what she'd agreed to until the questions began to come at her like flies to hamburgers out on a picnic table in the middle of August.

"What's the plan of action? This is Puerto Rico. Who will be your backup in case there's trouble? Will you be issued a weapon? Can you shoot to kill, if you have to?"

The last question wasn't something Callie had even considered. Could she? Would it go that far? What had she just agreed to? These were all relevant questions, and Callie now realized that she should have talked to Dom before accepting this assignment. But her level of commitment to this particular assignment was overwhelmingly strong. She wasn't going to back out. It felt like a defining moment for her; something that would be for the greater good, allowing her to discover new parts of herself.

Callie expressed those feelings to Dom, and although his final comments were ones of concern, they were a testament to the man she'd fallen in love with. "Darlin'," Dom said with a sigh, "I'm really not comfortable with you putting yourself in harm's way, especially given that I can't be there in case something goes wrong. Having said that, I understand your need to do it, because I've been on that side of the fence. So I guess if you're leaving in two days, we'd better make every minute count until then."

Then he took his hat off, revealing his beautiful jet-black hair, pulled her as close as physically possible and totally surrounding her with his strong arms. And the kiss... it was one she'd never forget. He had never kissed her that way before. It felt as if he was either begging her to stay or saying good-bye.

"Wow, Cowboy! Where did that come from?" Callie said as she caught her breath.

"It came from the deepest part of my heart, where you live, Darlin'."

"And I felt it in the deepest part of mine, Dom."

And with that, Dom smiled, put his hat back on and got up

from the blanket. "It's time to make this a night we'll never forget. Let's saddle up the ponies. We've got a date with a few stars in our own little slice of heaven."

Callie didn't know what he meant, but she was sure that whatever he had up his sleeve would be nothing other than spectacular. As Dom helped Callie onto DD and she took the reins, she looked back to take a mental snapshot of this beautiful place. Every day with this man just seemed to get better.

Dom saddled up and they rode the horses deeper into the woods for another hour or so, until another clearing appeared in Callie's view; this time, with the outline of a rooftop in the distance, not just foliage. As they got closer, Dom said, "Here's that slice of heaven I told you about." He told her that this was a special project he'd been working on in conjunction with his dude ranch concept.

It was a mid-sized log cabin with a wraparound porch, complete with a wooden swing and tables and chairs, and a hitching post and watering trough for the horses to one side. As they dismounted and walked up the cobblestone walkway, Callie could see a wood-burnished sign hanging from the front porch. It read, "Lovers' Lodge." Dom had designed it as a couples retreat, and as they walked through the front door, she understood what he meant when he said it was a slice of heaven. It was very similar to the cabin in Ruidoso she loved so much, except that it was smaller, more suited for two people.

Looking around, Callie was awestruck by the spa bath with his-and-hers towels, soaps, and robes, a bedroom with a beautiful four-poster bed surrounded by sheer white curtains and a table and two chairs for an intimate meal, an eat-in kitchen, a completely stocked wine closet, and of course, a gazebo-covered hot tub, with a small lap pool down a few steps from the back porch.

As usual, Dom had spared no details. You could stay in this retreat for months and never want to leave. Callie stepped out to the back porch to take in the beauty of the surroundings and noticed a truck parked on a gravel road off to the side.

"Hey, Babe ..." Callie called to Dom, who was opening a bottle of wine. "... where does this road go?"

Dom stepped out and handed Callie her glass and said, "To the ranch," giving her a wink, as if he'd pulled a prank on her.

"What? Why didn't we just drive here, then?" Callie asked, almost immediately realizing the answer.

"But we'd have missed a memory or two doing that, right?"

"Yes. That was sort of a dumb question, wasn't it?"

"No, not dumb at all, Darlin'. For us and couples like us, the slow and less beaten path is the most beautiful. For others, alternatives are necessary."

They finished their first glass of wine, and Dom said he'd

be right back, stepping back inside. When he returned, he said, "How about we ask the wine to join us for a bubble bath? The water is filling in the tub."

"I'd love a bath right now."

"Great! We'll be out in plenty of time for our final sunset of the year."

"Oh, wow. It is the final one, isn't it? I can't wait to see the colors you've ordered up for us from here."

It was clear to Callie that Dom enjoyed taking care of her, but she'd never experienced a bath like this. He started by helping her into the tub and sat down on the stool beside the tub to wash her hair, which came with a cowboy head massage. Then he joined her in the tub and they took turns lathering and rinsing each other off while they talked and sipped their wine. The trip to Puerto Rico hadn't come up even once, and Callie still wasn't sure how either of them was handling it. It didn't seem to be of consequence at the moment, though. She was just going to be in the moment, with him, enjoying Lovers' Lodge.

With bath time over as the water cooled off, it was time to prep for shish kebab on the grill. There was a turtle cheesecake thawing in the fridge, which would be perfect for dessert later. But in the meantime, the sun was beginning to descend into the trees, so Callie and Dom went back outside to watch the splendor.

From sunset to sunset, no two can ever compare. On this

last night of the year, the colors seemed to be unique, with more pink than usual for winter. They were all beautiful in their own way, but this one was special, for sure. Callie couldn't help but think about the sunset that had introduced her to Dom and be saddened by this one, their last one together for a while. She reminded herself that it would only be for a short time, and she reached over and gave Dom a kiss as the sun said its final good-bye for the night.

Dinner was as amazing as always, as was a swim and a half hour in the hot tub to warm up from the cool winter night. After toweling off and changing into dry clothes, Callie and Dom returned to the deck for a late-night dessert and coffee. At about 11:30, Callie heard a pop in the distance and then saw a flash of light in the sky, followed by more pops, and suddenly the sky was dancing with colors.

"Dom, look! Fireworks!" Callie exclaimed, her eyes almost mirroring the illuminated sky.

"Just another slice of heaven I ordered for you, Darlin'. It's our own special show," he said, grinning like a little boy who'd just hit his first homerun.

For the next half hour, they smiled and oohed and aahed as the display intensified exponentially until the end. And then, as the colors gave the sky back to the stars at the stroke of midnight, Callie and Dom sealed the beginning of the new year with a kiss and a toast to a continued love and life together. After dessert and coffee was finished, they retreated to the bedroom for a night of intimacy like they'd never shared. Callie knew that the coming year was going to present challenges to their relationship, but she refused to allow those thoughts to steal one second of the memories she was making with Dom now.

The morning sun's warmth appeared on Callie's face and caused her to open her sleepy eyes. She didn't want to move, but she felt a strange void and rolled over in the bed to find an empty place where Dom had been. She didn't hear any noise, but she smelled the fresh brew of coffee. Expecting to see him in the kitchen, she got up and went to the next room, but he wasn't there. She called out to him, but got no response. She put her slippers on and checked out front, back and to the side, but he was nowhere to be found.

*Hmm*, she thought, *where could he be?* She decided to have coffee on the deck, grabbing her warm white robe and sitting down. As she looked to the side of the house where the truck had been parked, she realized it was gone and began to freak out a bit. He hadn't mentioned going anywhere, and he'd been awfully quiet about her trip since they'd talked about it. Was he really okay with all of this, or was he upset with her? Surely he hadn't left her there alone out of anger.

Her insecurities were beginning to get the best of her after about 20 minutes of the uncertainty of his whereabouts. Appropriately timed to prevent a full-on freak-out moment, she heard the sound of tires crackling on the gravel road and quickly walked to the front porch to assure herself that it was Dom, and it was.

He got out of the truck and said, "Oh, you're up? I wanted to let you sleep in, but I had to run an errand."

"What kind of errand? It's a holiday, and we have everything we need here. You scared me. I thought all kinds of horrible things when I woke up and you weren't here, Cowboy."

Dom said, "I'm sorry, Darlin'. I was up all night thinking about you and Puerto Rico. I know I said I'd support you on this, but I just needed to work things out in my own head. I'm really worried about you doing this. So I left before sunrise and went to my supply room at the ranch and brought some things back for you. If you're going to do this, I want to be sure you can handle things if they get out of hand. It would just make me feel better. So today, I'm going to teach you a few tricks of the trade. First up, a weapon and a lesson in shooting."

Callie was nearly speechless, which didn't happen often, but when got over her disbelief of what Dom had just said, she flung her arms around him and said, "Just when I think I know how much I love you, you surprise me again."

Dom simply responded, "I will never stop doing that,

Callie."

After a quick breakfast of blueberry bagels and cream cheese, Callie got dressed and they got in the truck for some good old-fashioned firearms practice. When they got out of the truck a few miles into the woods, Dom set up random paint can targets and came back to hand Callie a handgun in a holster. It was a Sig Sauer P238 .380 semiautomatic. Dom explained that it was his pick for her because it was compact enough to conceal, there was very little recoil, and he wanted her to carry it at all times.

With a few preliminary instructions out of the way, Dom said, "All right. Let's see what you've got. Can you hit that target off to the left?"

Callie fired off the first shot, then another and another, hitting the target each time. When she stopped and turned to look at Dom, he had a look of amazement on his face.

"Have you been keeping secrets from me, Darlin'?

"No, not really. I grew up with guns in the house, and Daddy took me out a few times for target practice, but I haven't picked up a gun in years."

"Well, you're a natural, and I think we can move on to something else. Two things to remember in the field: If your life is in jeopardy, make the first shot count, because you may not get a second one off; secondly, your survival instinct has to trump all other emotions when there's a living, breathing person who's your target.  Paint cans don't have mamas, but they can't kill you either."

Callie packed up those words and put them away for safekeeping.  Even though they'd never talked about his time in the field, Dom clearly had experience in this arena and was giving her sage advice.  They continued on with a little more target practice and then headed back to the lodge for more serious conversation about the trip.

Grabbing two bottled waters and sitting down on the sofa in the living room, Dom brought out a metal lockbox, opened it up and pulled out a tiny black metal circular object.  It looked like a button battery you'd put in a watch, but Dom explained that it was a tracking device, and Callie would insert it into the lining of her purse.  He gave her a few more and told her that she should put one in her car and she could attach one to the back of her wristwatch.

Dom spent the next few hours going over as many field tips as he could throw at Callie, adding that he'd have something special shipped to her in DC at the training camp.  He was going to have it designed especially for her, but it would take a few days to make that happen.

It was finally time for lunch, and both Callie and Dom were starving.  They ate a nice salad, throwing in the leftover veggies, steak and shrimp from the night before, cozying up on the sofa afterwards. In less than 24 hours, they'd be separated. This was going to be difficult for Callie, but she hoped she'd be busy enough that she wouldn't have time to think about how much she missed her lovely cowboy. She'd learned more about Dom in the last 24 hours than she'd known in the last six months. They had bonded in a way they never would have, had this opportunity not presented itself, and it had made their relationship stronger.

It was New Year's Day, and while most people were watching football and getting over hangovers from their celebrations the night before, it was time for Callie to go home and finish packing. She desperately wanted to stay here with Dom, but he must have sensed her level of anxiety and had his own similar feelings, because he hopped up from the sofa about 5:00 p.m., and said, "Well, Darlin', why don't we head over to your house and I can help you pack. I'll drop you at the airport in the morning and see you off to your exciting island adventure."

Could this man be real? Yes, he was real, and he was all hers. Together, they made sense in a sometimes senseless world. All of the things and people they'd each lost along their way to each other seemed to fade with every passing day they spent together.

"First one out to the truck owes the other a Corona," said Callie, running to her purse and overnight bag by the front door. And Dom let her win... this time. Several hours later, Callie was so grateful that Dom had come with her to help her pack. He knew exactly what she should take and what to leave at home, and she got to spend these last few extra hours with him before she left. He even offered to come by the house while she was gone to water the plants and pick up her mail and newspaper; something else she hadn't thought of.

Their last night together was one of almost complete silence, along with the trip to the airport. Ordinarily, that would have bothered Callie, but somehow, in this situation, it felt calming, giving her time to just be, without overanalyzing anything. The private jet was waiting at the scheduled time inside a hangar on the far end of the Austin airport, away from the hustle and bustle of the main airport.

Dom got her bags out and carried them to the plane, handing them to the copilot and stopping to hug and kiss Callie one final time before watching her fly off and disappear above the clouds on this brisk January morning.

Whispering in Callie's ear, he simply said, "Vaya con dios, Darlin'. I love you."

"I love you more, Cowboy. Lasso an Austin sunset for me."

As the Learjet left the runway and aimed its nose for the heavens, Callie wiped the tears from her eyes. It was time to show the rest of the world what she was made of, and she was ready.

# Chapter 3: Duplicity

**_San Juan, PR, January 2_**

It had been weeks since Mercedes had heard anything from the feds about helping her out of the enormous mess she'd made of her life, and she was starting to get really frustrated. At her wit's end, she was pondering the thought of running, which had always been her natural instinct. But she'd done that before, and that's why she was in this predicament. A few seconds after thinking about this, she heard the faint ring tone of the cell phone she'd been sent by Agent Kendrick, and quickly ran to answer his call.

"Hello?"

"Mercedes, this is Frank Kendrick. Plans are underway on your case. Hold tight. An agent will be in Puerto Rico by the 15th of this month and will reach out to you."

"Oh, thank God," Mercedes said.

"Everything will be just fine. Keep doing what you're doing. It won't be much longer," Kendrick said reassuringly, as he hung up on his end.

*Finally!* Mercedes thought to herself. She'd spent the entire holiday season trying to be patient and enjoy some part of it, but there was this awful sense of dread that she just couldn't shake. The sound of Kendrick's voice had calmed her doubts and fears, or at least kept them at bay for the moment. She could be patient for a little while longer. A two-week trial would be starting at 10:00 a.m., and she was hopeful that her nighttime personal services wouldn't be required during the course of it.

Arriving at the courthouse an hour early, she hid out in her office until 20 minutes prior to the proceedings. She didn't trust any of the court reporters in this courthouse. They all seemed nice enough to her face, but she'd heard most of them gossiping about other women. In light of that, she wasn't going to risk letting them on the inside of her secret life. She had no one on this stupid island that she could trust, but she was hoping that was about to change. She wondered how someone could be surrounded by so many people and simultaneously be so lonely.

Court was about to begin, and a new lawyer from the states approached with his business card, introducing himself.

"Good morning, Madame Court Reporter. I'm Jake Fresby, here on the Menendez matter."

"Good morning, Mr. Fresby," Mercedes said, extending her hand for a shake. "Mercedes Cruz. Welcome to Puerto Rico. It's very nice to meet you."

As the young attorney walked off, she smiled on the outside, but she smirked on the inside, thinking to herself that he had no idea that *Madame Court Reporter* took on a completely different meaning for her. She couldn't wait to walk away from this life and all that it entailed, never to hear that title again.

### *Langley, Virginia, January 3*

Callie's alarm went off at 4:00 a.m., because arrangements had been made for her to be picked up and taken to the FBI's undercover agents training camp just outside Washington, DC. She'd be there for an intensive boot camp personally designed for her and her operation. She'd be trained on everything from firearms to tactical operations to physical, and although she was nervous, she was up for it.

Although Callie wasn't a young woman, she was physically in the best shape of her life, and she knew she could manage the firearms training. The real challenge was going to be tactical operations. There was so much to learn in a really short amount of time, but she was confident she'd get through it and be on her way to San Juan with the tools necessary to complete her assignment.

The first day was forms day; something Callie had come to detest in the latter part of her life. The government in action; everything in proper order and disclaimers everywhere. After she'd signed her name in blood on multiple documents, it was time for them to draw some from her arm, just to be sure there were no physical problems she was unaware of.

The rest of the 12-hour day was spent in physical exercises, meaning gauntlets and endurance contests. This was intense, and at the end of the day, Callie was completely wiped out. She would need plenty of carbs to keep up this pace. Pasta was on the dinner menu before going back to the hotel for a Jacuzzi bath and a date with the really comfortable mattress.

When she arrived at the hotel at the end of the day, the front desk said she had a package. It was the package Dom had told her he was sending, and she couldn't wait to see what was inside. She pushed the elevator button a number of times in an effort to hurry it up, but of course, the only thing that had ever done was make her feel better about waiting for it.

Once in her room, Callie threw her purse down, hopped on the bed and ripped open the package. Inside was a small red leather jewelry box reminiscent of the one Dom had given her at the beginning of their sweet romance. The top had the same branded "C" monogram surrounded by a rope. She opened the box to reveal a beautiful sterling silver necklace with a large pendant in the shape of the Texas star. There was a large, sparkling ruby in the center of the star. It was quite a piece of work, and it was signature Dom.

While she loved the necklace, especially because it was her favorite color and from her favorite state and her favorite cowboy, she had expected something that would help her with the assignment, and this didn't quite seem to fit the bill for that. Looking further into the package, there was an envelope.

*Of course,* she thought. *My cowboy is all about the sweetness of the details.*

The note read: "Callie, the necklace has a dual purpose. The first is to let you know that you are my shining Lone Star. The second is something you can't see. There's a tiny camera in the center of the ruby. That camera is my eye into your world. Press on the back of the ruby, and it will begin to send a live feed to my secure station. I will be watching, and if trouble appears, so will I. All my love, Dom."

This man! He really did love her, and she trusted him with her life. Even though Callie was confident she could take care of herself if push came to shove, it was reassuring to know that Dom was watching. But he was in Texas, and that's a long flight from Austin. It would be hard for him to come riding up on Yin Yang to rescue her from there. Regardless, he was on her A-team, and that was huge.

Callie spent the next few days impressing the male agents with her firearms skills. No matter the weapon, she aced the course. Next came the tactical exercises. They were designed to teach her how to get in and out of an operation successfully without being compromised, and albeit new to her skill set, she was a quick study and completed the course to their satisfaction.

The final two days of Callie's training encompassed setting up her alias, educating her on the specifics of the assignment, and handing out all the superspy tech gear. There were so many handy gadgets in her arsenal now. It had been the most intense ten days of her life, but she was armed with everything she needed to take on the Puerto Rican project, appropriately code-named "Duplicity."

Callie Fletcher, a Texas court reporter, was now an undercover court reporter named Elizabeth Wells, investigating a Puerto Rican federal judge for pimping out a courtesan who was pretending to be a court reporter. Geez, if her daddy could see her now! If there had ever been a more duplicitous circumstance, Callie was unaware of it. *This would make a nice plot for a movie,* she thought to herself.

Her flight to San Juan was scheduled for the next morning at 6:00 a.m., so bedtime would be early, but a little laundry was due first. She wanted to talk to her favorite guy before she hit the pillows, and then her kids. She hadn't told them anything about this trip because, number one, it was top secret, and number two, she knew they'd be worried.

She had taken the time to write a letter to them and ensure all of her affairs were in order, just in case, but all of that was in a sealed envelope inside her safe. Both kids had the combination to it and would know what to do in the event something went south. If there was one thing she had learned from her husband Mike's death, it was to properly plan for an unexpected life circumstance.

To put a more positive spin on her thoughts, she was going to pour herself a glass of wine and call Dom. There was nothing more soothing than listening to the sound of his deep voice, and she was anxious to update him on her boot camp success and thank him for the designer Texas spycam necklace.

Callie plopped down in the comfy hotel room chair by the window, glass in hand, and slid the heavy coral curtains back to enjoy the view from the 10th floor. She could see the lights of DC in the distance, illuminating the sky. This was no Texas sky, but it was beautiful nonetheless. Although she couldn't see her favorite two stars twinkling above, she could feel their presence.

Just as she was about to push the "Dom" button on her cell phone, she nearly dropped her glass of wine when she heard the familiar ringtone she'd assigned to him, *Cowboy, Take Me Away*. She answered immediately, still laughing out loud.

"Having a party without me, Darlin'?"

"Ha ha! There's no such thing, Babe. Did you bug my room without telling me? I was literally just about to push the button to call you, and you beat me to it."

"Spies never tell, Callie," he said, jokingly.

"Court reporters don't either," Callie said with a little giggle.

After the first sip of wine, they began to talk about the week and how much they missed each other, realizing this would be the last conversation they'd be able to have until her return home. The reality began to sink in, analogous to the final curing of a concrete slab. There was no turning back, and Callie would be on her own — something that sounded okay in theory, but was very scary for them both, now that the rubber was about to meet the road.

Dom reassured Callie that everything would be just fine, and she let him know how safe she felt knowing that he would be watching, even if it was from such a long distance. It gave her a sense of security that she didn't have with her handler, Kendrick.

As the two said their final "I love yous" and hung up the phone, Callie began to panic a bit, but poured another glass of wine for a little liquid courage, conjuring up that inner strength she was born with. It was time to call the kids, and that would be a welcome distraction. She would have to avoid talking about herself so as not to let anything slip out, but that hadn't been a problem since they'd moved away from home.

The calls with the kids went well until she told them that she'd be out of pocket for a bit; that she was working on a case that would keep her occupied for a while. They didn't ask questions, but they knew it wasn't anything unusual to go for periods of time without talking to her. And with that last bit of joy out of the way, it was time to sleep, and then focus.

Given Callie's anxiety over her trip to Puerto Rico and the uncertainty of the events that might unfold, Callie fell asleep surprisingly quickly, and the alarm went off what seemed like seconds later. It was D-Day, and Callie's stomach was doing a number on her while she was having her morning coffee in the dimly lit hotel room. She decided to take a Valerian, a natural supplement she'd given her son as a teenager for his weak stomach. That seemed to calm both her stomach and her mood, and she was off to the lobby to meet the car which would take her to another private airstrip.

It was a brisk, clear day in the DC area, hopefully allowing for a smooth trek across the Atlantic into San Juan. Callie was grateful in this case not to have to deal with getting through airport security, being cramped into a metal box full of screaming babies and uncomfortable seats. Private jets were definitely the way to go for travel. *Dom is going to have to buy one of these for the ranch*, she thought to herself as she boarded her heavenly carriage.

Wheels up and into the skies, Callie began to think about her last trip to this beautiful island in the Caribbean. She'd gone there for ten days to sub in federal court for her sweet friend, Laney, while Laney and her husband Trey went on a cruise. Laney paid for the entire trip, and Callie would be doing realtime hookups for the judge there. There was a full week's trial set, and

Laney walked Callie through everything regarding the court system, food, walking the dog and driving around the city.

Driving in Puerto Rico presented its own set of challenges. Callie quickly discovered why there was a speed limit of 45 miles per hour on the interstate system there. The use of a blinker to change lanes was actually a signal to other drivers to speed up. Callie had decided that it must have been some sort of native custom, but got on board with it immediately.

Laney had told Callie that the week should go fairly smoothly and the weather was set to be beautiful. That hadn't turned out to be the case, however. The first day at work, there was a change in courtrooms, requiring Callie's equipment and hookups to be restarted elsewhere, just minutes before selecting a jury, and tech support was in another courtroom. Callie had begun to freak out when the judge's laptop wouldn't reach the hard-wired cable, and she'd been told that the judge was particular about the placement of his laptop.

Looking to the female courtroom deputy, Callie had asked for help... with no response, zero, as if she was invisible. Rude behavior wasn't a rarity in Callie's life, but rude behavior in an unfamiliar place, where she knew no one, left her without any recourse except to wait for tech support. They eventually came and the trial was off and running, but that experience had left Callie feeling out of sorts.

Just a few minutes before the afternoon session on that first day, the courtroom security officer had remarked to Callie, "You came back!" Callie had grinned and said, "Of course," at which point he explained that another visiting reporter had left and gone back to the States after a lunch break. Given her morning's experience, Callie certainly understood why that might have happened, but she wasn't one to renege on a commitment.

Once the rhythm of her new environment set in, the week had been like any other. The high of the day came when a young, blond-haired, blue-eyed male federal prosecutor came walking into the courtroom and introduced himself. And when Callie shook his hand and they began to exchange backgrounds, his eyes lit up and he mentioned he used to work in Mississippi. As they began to talk further, he told her he knew her dad, which had made Callie feel some sense of home. Jokingly, she'd always told her dad that she could never go anywhere and get into trouble because everywhere she traveled, someone always knew him.

The low of that time happened that same day at about 5:00 p.m., when court was out and the monsoon came. Callie's little handheld umbrella was completely useless. Fat, sideways walls of water pelted her all the way to the uncovered parking lot. The only part of her that wasn't wet was her hair.

She'd decided to wait until the rain let up to drive the three or so miles back to Laney's apartment, but that turned out to be a huge mistake.  The rain stopped just as suddenly as it had started, but the roads were beginning to fill up with people and flooding waters.  With no public transportation in San Juan, gridlock was eminent, and aggressive drivers took over the roads.  It took nearly an hour and a half to get back to the safety of the apartment, and Callie was grateful that the following day was a Puerto Rican holiday.

The week of work and stressful driving had ended, and a couple of the local court reporters called and invited Callie to dinner out, which was a welcome kindness.  Funny enough, dinner was at an American chain restaurant at an enormous three-story mall in San Juan, so it felt even closer to home than meeting the young attorney.

Laney and Trey returned over the weekend, and Laney took Callie on a tour of Casa Bacardi, complimentary rum included, a drive-through tour of Old San Juan, and later, they met Trey for dinner at a popular local steakhouse.  The trip was an amazing experience, with just a few bumps in the road, but one thing that Callie was certain of is that there was no place like home.  Puerto Rico was nothing like Austin.

Callie's trip down memory lane took up pretty much the entirety of her flight from DC to San Juan, and the pilot had just announced his descent when she came out of it.  *Here we go,* Callie thought.  *Get your game face on.*  The screeching of the wheels and the whirring of the brakes pressing into the rubber caused Callie's heart to begin to pound. She thought this might be a good time to take another one of those Valerian capsules. This time around, San Juan would need to be a distraction-free zone.

Disembarking from the comfort of the jet, Callie had to remove her winter jacket. Contrary to Virginia, it was a balmy 80 degrees in San Juan, and the sun was shining gloriously in the cloud-free sky. It was as gorgeous as she had remembered. A car was waiting to take her to her new digs, and she was anxious to see where she would be living. She was now Elizabeth Wells, and she'd have to remember to answer to that.

Although her cover would have her returning to the same federal courthouse, it had been nearly ten years since her one-week visit, and she would be holding a new name, donning a beautiful red wig cut much shorter than her natural style, and wearing glasses. Frank had arranged for her to be credentialed and set up to temporarily sub for a judge, which turned out to be easier than normal, because there was always an empty reporter seat to be filled in that district.

Thankfully, her new place was within one block of the courthouse, and she wouldn't have to drive to work; something that was extremely appealing, no matter what it looked like on the inside. But when her driver accompanied her up the elevator to the sixth floor with her luggage and opened the front door, her eyes widened in amazement. *Geez, the feds know how to make a girl feel welcome,* she thought. A small but well-appointed kitchen was just steps from a covered, Mexican-tiled balcony, and the apartment was beautifully decorated with casual furnishings.

Callie's personal cover story was that she was there to make extra money for a very expensive, experimental medical procedure for her husband, who was dying from liver cancer, and the insurance company was refusing to pay. Desperate to save his life, she needed the extra income from the daily copy orders which were frequently requested in the courts here. She would reach out to and befriend Mercedes, bringing her into her confidence and desperation over her dilemma, without disclosing her true role at first. The primary goal was to ascertain the veracity of Mercedes' character and allegations she was making.

If Callie could confirm that the allegations warranted further investigation, she would then let Mercedes know she was there to help her, and the two could begin gathering the necessary evidence. Otherwise, Callie would return home, her fact-finding mission being complete. This made perfect sense to Callie. The FBI wasn't going to just presume the guilt of a federal judge and dignitary on the mere allegations of someone they had no history with who could have an ax to grind.

If this "Madame" pretending to be a court reporter was

defrauding the legal system and trying to make her judge a scapegoat, Callie would stop her in her tracks. There was no way she'd let someone take advantage of the system she valued most in her life. But if the judge was, indeed, guilty of taking advantage of this young woman and abusing the serious responsibility he was appointed by the President and Congress to fulfill for life, she would find the evidence to support him being removed from the bench and brought to justice.

Unpacking just as expeditiously as she had packed the night before, Callie went to the fridge to see what needed to be added to her grocery list and found it to be completely stocked with all of her favorites. How did they do that? Well, it was on one of those pesky forms she'd had to fill out at the beginning of boot camp. She was suddenly a little more appreciative of the time she'd spent filling out that particular one.

She began to brew a pot of coffee, then stepped out onto the deck to enjoy her last evening of quiet time before arriving at her new post in the morning. After a warm bath and a nice dinner salad with fresh veggies, grilled chicken and a bottled water, Callie began to feel the jetlag kicking in and made her way to the most comfortable mattress she'd ever slept on. The bedroom was tiny, but the seafoam paint on the walls was inviting enough to make her feel welcome. In just minutes, her brain gave way to her body and she drifted off to sleep.

### U.S. District Court, San Juan, PR, January 14

Mercedes drove into the parking lot a little early to get a jump on the morning motions and noticed a redheaded woman walking up the sidewalk to the employee entrance of the courthouse. She hadn't seen this woman before and wondered who she might be. As she entered the back doors, she overheard the security guards giving the redhead directions to the personnel office.

*Hmm*, she thought, *she's probably a new law clerk from the States*. Shrugging the thoughts off as the redhead got on the elevator, she couldn't help but notice how strikingly beautiful the woman was. Whoever she was, it didn't matter. The only thing that mattered at this moment was getting off this island. She had been unbelievably patient, but her patience was wearing really thin now. Something needed to happen soon, or she'd have to take matters into her own hands.

The courtroom began to fill up with lawyers around 8:30 a.m. It was another boring motion day for Mercedes, but she would only be working until noon. Franco had some family obligation to attend to, and she was happy that she didn't have to be in a room with him for the entire day. As he stepped onto the bench and the courtroom deputy announced his presence, Mercedes refused to look at him, lowered her eyes and began moving her fingers across the keys of her steno machine. *Another day of deceit*, she thought, sighing quietly.

The proceedings were in full swing, and Mercedes finally looked to the back of the courtroom and noticed the woman she'd seen earlier that morning. As their eyes met briefly, the woman smiled at her, but Mercedes quickly lowered her eyes, never changing the blank expression on her face. Smiles didn't come without costing her something these days, so she gave them out infrequently. Out of curiosity, however, she looked up ten minutes later, and the woman was no longer there.

The judge announced adjournment for the day, and Mercedes gathered up her things and left for the parking lot. It was time for a beer and a nap. Sleeping was her only escape from reality, it seemed. But as she walked down the sidewalk to the parking lot, the woman was just steps in front of her. *All right! That's enough of that! I have to know who this woman is.* And with that thought, she hurried her steps to catch up to the woman.

Jumping right to the point, Mercedes asked, "New here?"

"Yes," Callie responded. "Liz Wells. I'm a court reporter from the States, filling in temporarily. And you are?"

"Mercedes Cruz. I noticed you in my courtroom this morning."

"Yes, I was there to observe the proceedings, just to become familiar with the process here. I don't actually sit in court until tomorrow."

"I see," Mercedes said, satisfying her curiosity. Thinking to herself that this was just another person within the system she couldn't trust, she added, "Well, nice to meet you. I hope you enjoy your stay here."

"Do you have any suggestions for lunch? I'm not familiar with the area, and I'm starving."

Not really wanting to have more conversation, but realizing it wouldn't hurt to make a suggestion or two, Mercedes offered up a few nearby local restaurants she liked.

"Great! Thank you so much! Are you free for lunch? And if so, would you mind joining me? I'm feeling a little out of my element, and it would be nice to have the company."

The invitation caught Mercedes off guard, and without thinking it through, the word "sure" came out instantaneously. *Oh, crap! What did I just do?* Mercedes thought. Disgusted with herself that her need to please had just won again, she threw that thought to the side by telling herself that it was just lunch. What would be the harm in it? She'd just keep the conversation light and away from the details of her life.

The two of them then proceeded to walk down a few blocks to Juan's. It had the best fajitas and draught beer in town. It was a quaint little place, and it wasn't extremely busy. There was an umbrella-covered table available on the patio, and no one was out there. They were seated and ordered food right away.

While they were waiting for their fajitas, Mercedes began to ask more questions about the woman's life in the States. She was asking the general get-to-know-you questions that everyone asks when they first meet. Not that she cared about any of this, but it was filler conversation. Where was she from? Was she married? Did she have kids? Where did she grow up?

What unfolded during the course of that conversation was more than Mercedes could have planned for, however. She began to feel sorry for this woman, who had come to San Juan out of desperation. This beautiful woman who had been smiling on the outside was very sad on the inside. Though the details were very different in their lives, the framework seemed to mirror Mercedes' circumstances, and by the end of lunch, Mercedes was hooked, connected, like it or not. Her heart had become softened by the love this woman had for her family and the desperation that had brought her to this island.

"Thank you for having lunch with me and listening. I needed to unburden for a few minutes, and I'm so grateful for the kind ear," Liz said.

As they got up to go their separate ways, Mercedes simply responded, "I've never known the love you enjoy. I pray that you don't have to give that up. If I can do anything to help while you're here, let me know."

Mercedes watched as Liz walked away, thinking that she'd come away from lunch without sharing any of her secrets, but gaining an understanding of how small her plight seemed to be in comparison to what she'd discovered about her new acquaintance. She'd spent months wishing she had someone else's life, but now she just wanted to keep her own and make it better than it was.

### Later that night, Callie's apartment...

Callie picked up the secure cell as it rang and reported to Kendrick that Operation Duplicity had gotten off to a successful start. She'd made contact with the source of the tip and had begun to secure her trust. One of the key things Callie had noticed during her observations of Mercedes in the courtroom was that she was most definitely not a steno reporter. She reminded Callie of one of those random film extras, flapping her fingers across the keys in a way that was a telltale sign of pretense to even beginning reporters.

Regardless of whether Mercedes' allegations against her judge were true, this particular part of her story was fact. Those outside the profession wouldn't think it would be possible to pull off such a feat, especially while providing realtime to the judge, but Callie knew it was possible and pointed that out to Kendrick.

Technology inside the profession had come so far that a reporter could be in the courtroom writing, and editors and proofreaders could be outside the courtroom, hooked up via the Internet, and all of them could be getting an audio and video feed, working on the transcript at the same time. In light of that, it would be easy for a remote reporter to be writing on her machine and sending the feed through to the judge's computer, allowing Mercedes to simply sit in her chair and look pretty, faking her way through the day.

Callie had always been good at reading people, and she was able to gain their trust by sharing intimate details about herself first. This came quite naturally in her personal life, so it complemented her undercover work nicely. Although lying didn't come naturally, it was easier when the goal was one of bringing someone to justice.

Kendrick was pleased with the results so far and told her to keep up the good work. After ending the call, she devised a plan for the next few days. What she'd learned about Mercedes so far was that she was eager to help. She was rough around the edges, but a softy on the inside. Callie would gain Mercedes' trust and find the truth by allowing Mercedes to believe she was helping. In Callie's experience, the way to discovering a woman's deepest, darkest secrets was to give up some of your own. And if desperation, tears, and a plea for help were added to the mix, very few human beings could resist the urge to come to the rescue. It was the most basic form of feminine manipulation.

Not wanting to risk spooking Mercedes by attempting to bond with her too quickly, Callie decided to give the relationship time to bloom normally. Too much too soon was never a good thing. She purposely kept herself to work and home for the next two days. Work was the same in every court, it seemed. San Juan was no different. People spoke, and Callie listened and took their testimony.

On Thursday after court, an opportunity presented itself. Sitting in her office, Callie noticed Mercedes pass by her office, bag in hand, on the way out. She scooped up her purse, locked her door and caught up to her standing in wait for the elevator. She noticed Mercedes hit the button several times in exactly the way she had done it and couldn't help giggling, and Mercedes turned around and smiled at her.

This was the first time Callie had seen her smile. The young woman was clearly troubled by something. It was time to get a little closer to find out what was at the root of her sadness. As the doors to the elevator opened and they both stepped on, Callie said, "Long day, huh? I was about to see if I could find a drink somewhere."

Callie was going to extend another invitation to Mercedes, but to Callie's surprise, Mercedes asked if she could join her. This was definitely a step in the right direction. It meant that Mercedes was slowly opening the door to let Callie in.

"I know a great place by the water just a short drive from here. We can take my car if you want," Mercedes offered.

"That would be fantastic." Callie replied. "I haven't learned the rules of the road here yet, and I live close enough to work to walk. You're sure it's not too much trouble to drop me off at my place afterwards?"

"Not at all," Mercedes said.

Pulling up to Oceano's, Callie almost teared up. It was a much smaller and jazzier version of Shenanigans where she'd met Dom. She'd been so busy and focused on Operation Duplicity that she hadn't allowed herself to think about just how much she missed him. The view from this place was like nothing she'd ever seen, though, and thoughts of Dom shifted back to the business at hand. The water in the Caribbean was just so majestic. You could see through to the bottom, especially from the top deck of the restaurant. The blues and greens looked as if they had been painted on a canvas by the hands of God.

Opting for a table outside to make the most of the spectacular view and to forget about the drudgery of the court day, Callie and Mercedes began to talk more. And with the alcohol flowing, Mercedes began to open up, and Callie took full advantage of the effects of the Happy Hour by asking background questions.

"Are your parents still living? I lost my dad a few years ago, and I'm still having a hard time living a life without him."

Mercedes paused for a few seconds as her eyes saddened, finally responding, "My mommy died when I was 16, and my poppy disappeared a few months later. He went out for a bottle of whiskey and never came home."

Callie reached over and put her hand on top of Mercedes, saying, "I can't even imagine how afraid you must have been. Did you have any other family nearby?"

"No, and I was an only child. One of my schoolteachers must have sensed something was going on because she called CPS and they put me in an awful group home. It was a roof and free meals, but that was all. I made one friend there, who I'm still in touch with, though. She works with the federal government in the States."

Mercedes was really opening up, and Callie began to gain an understanding of the incredible loss this young woman had suffered at such a young age. Without adding anything to the conversation except a consoling smile, Callie simply listened as Mercedes continued to tell her story.

"As soon as I turned 18, I got a job in a bar and pretty quickly moved in with the owner, who was 20 years older. He seemed nice at first, but after a few months, he started hitting me on a regular basis. He'd say it wouldn't happen again, but it always did. I took it for years, but one day when he left to pick up an employee who needed a ride to work, I took off. I'd been socking a little money away; just enough to get me to a new place."

"I'm so glad that you got out of that horrible environment. It says a lot about your strength," Callie said.

Mercedes, bringing the topic to a halt, said, "Well, thanks. I'm not sure about that, but my past is something I don't like to talk about." And then she added, "I'll be right back. The rest room calls." Callie surmised that Mercedes must have realized that the alcohol was knocking down the fortress she'd built to protect her secrets, but she left so abruptly that she'd forgotten her purse.

*Perfect opportunity!* Callie thought, as she took a SIM card out of its case in her purse and inserted it into the empty slot in Mercedes' smartphone. This was an amazing listening device, and Mercedes would never know that it was recording every word she said, even when her phone was off. Almost as soon as she'd completed the task, Callie began to feel guilty about intruding on Mercedes' privacy, especially after Mercedes had just shared so much about her tumultuous youth. The guilt was dispelled quickly, however, because she realized she didn't really know if any of Mercedes' story was the truth.

Mercedes returned from the rest room and suggested that it was probably time to get back home because she had an early morning in court. Callie agreed, and with one last look at the beach, admiring the beauty of the bleached-white sand and the gentle rippling of the foaming waves doing their now-moonlit dance, she picked up her purse and walked towards Mercedes' car.

The trip back to Callie's apartment was awkwardly quiet, but when Callie opened the door to get out of the car, she simply said, "Thank you for the company, for trusting me enough to share your story, and for the opportunity to feel normal and forget about my worries for a few hours. See you in the trenches."

Mercedes smiled and said, "Ditto!"

On the drive back home, Mercedes continued to smile, thinking she'd found someone she could be herself around. There was something very calming and welcoming about Liz; so much so that she would have to be very careful with sharing too much more with her. A compadre was sure nice to have on this godforsaken island, though. Maybe she'd even invite her over for dinner over the weekend. *That would be such fun!* she thought. And then there it was... a glimmer of joy.

Back at Callie's apartment, it was time to make another field report to Kendrick. With a quick call to him about the evening and her successful placement of the SIM card, she hung up and went to bed. The combination of her day in court, the emotional rollercoaster of her outing with Mercedes, and the alcohol had left her feeling exhausted, so she decided to make an early night of it. She was getting closer to Mercedes, and hopefully Operation Duplicity would be shifting into high gear very soon.

Pulling the covers up over her shoulders and closing her eyes, she saw Dom's gorgeous smile. She missed him so much... all of him. She comforted herself by imagining his muscular arms around her, her head on his comfy, hair-free chest. And with that soothing thought, she drifted off to sleep.

The next morning, as she walked up the sidewalk to the courthouse, she was greeted by a smiling Mercedes, who was dressed in a beautiful wraparound, denim dress with a red tie and sash at the waist, but the red leather dress boots were what caused Callie's eyes to widen in delight.

"Good morning, Lady in Red Boots!" Callie said.

"Good morning, my new friend. Got coffee?" Mercedes said, giving Callie a knowing wink.

"Not enough," Callie replied. You?"

"Oh, sure. I'm pretty much immune to the stuff, but I don't get hangovers either. Maybe that means I drink too much, huh?"

"Well, it could be that you're just lucky. We'll go with that."

Mercedes didn't seem to hesitate as she extended a dinner invitation to Callie for Saturday night, asking if she'd be interested in homemade enchiladas and margaritas at her place, and Callie quickly replied with an excited, "I'd love to!"

"Awesome! Pick you up at 7:00 p.m.?"

"Can't wait to get my Mexican on! Can I bring anything?"

"Just your party mood," Mercedes replied.

"I'll unpack that tonight. Have a great day in court!"

The two then went to their respective courtrooms, and Callie was feeling extremely confident that her plan was working. Her day in court was a short one, ending at 2:00, and it was a welcome relief, giving her time for a late lunch and a much-needed nap.

Naps were something that Callie relished now, because they were rare. She often thought that she needed them so much as an adult because she refused to give in to them as a child. Naptime in elementary school was on a plastic foam mat on the floor. Lying on the floor between two of her friends had provided Callie with the irresistible temptation to talk, getting her into trouble daily. Maybe that early life lesson was the catalyst to the decision to become a court reporter. There was very little opportunity to talk; hence, very little opportunity to get into trouble.

With a light lunch of pomegranate-walnut salad and a refreshing two-hour nap in her rearview mirror, Callie poured a freshly brewed java, opened her FBI-issued laptop and opened up the app where the recordings of Mercedes were held. Scrolling through to the time period when Mercedes wasn't in court, Callie heard Mercedes talking to someone on the phone at around 11:00 p.m. about an upcoming masquerade ball. Although she couldn't hear the other end of the conversation, as Mercedes ended the call, Callie heard her say, "Damn! I don't want to do this anymore!! God, please help me." And it was this conversation that allowed Callie to begin the next phase of Operation Duplicity.

She would put it into action while having dinner with Mercedes on Saturday. She had almost all the necessary information to ascertain the truthfulness of Mercedes' allegations, but she needed a confession, and she needed it while Mercedes still believed that "Liz" was simply her newfound confidante.

Friday was a much longer day in court, and the proceedings didn't end until around 7:00 p.m. Even though Callie was worn to a frazzle, she decided to get into her car and navigate the few miles to the Mall of San Juan. It was as enormous as she'd remembered, and she just wanted to window shop and perhaps pick up some gifts for Dom and her kids for her return home. She really detested shopping for herself, but buying for others was always a joy.

After finding a few things for the family, Callie was in the mood for a burger and fries, so she drove through the McDonald's on the way home, got a soda from the fridge and sat outside on the deck to enjoy the cool ocean breeze. One day, she'd return here when she wasn't on some work gig and could spend time enjoying all the beauty, architecture and history that the island had to offer. Maybe she'd come back with Dom and the family. That would be nice. But until then, it was time to focus on her mission.

After hours of staring into the distance and listening to the traffic and the faint sounds of an accordion and bongos playing a festive, happy little tune somewhere nearby. The music stopped somewhere around 1:00 a.m., at which point Callie fell asleep, sitting on the chaise lounger on the deck.

The coqui frogs began their very loud serenade around 4:00 a.m., intruding into Callie's dreams and awakening her. She couldn't believe she'd fallen asleep on the deck, but she was now wide awake. So instead of going to bed, she got up and made a fresh pot of coffee, deciding to watch the San Juan sunrise. She would need to take a power nap later in the day, because she had a feeling that this night with Mercedes was going to be one for the books.

Callie spent the day doing laundry and running errands and picked up a bottle of wine as a gift for Mercedes. She took her power nap around 4:00, showered and changed, and was ready when Mercedes texted to say she was in the parking lot at around 6:45.

Mercedes smiled as Callie got into the car and said excitedly, "Hi, Liz! Are you ready to get the fiesta started?"

"Absolutely!" Callie replied. "I know we were planning on margaritas, but I got this amazing white zin for you as a thank-you for the invitation. I seriously need some girl time."

"Aww, you didn't have to do that, but it was so nice of you! I'll accept it, but only if you agree to drink it with me."

"Of course. I rarely turn down an invitation for wine with a friend."

It took about a half hour to get to Mercedes' apartment building, which to Callie's surprise, was in a more affluent neighborhood than most single court reporters could have afforded in San Juan. It was in a gated community of Puntas Las Marias, and when Callie walked in the front door of this beautiful, very large and luxurious condo, she could see the ocean from every angle.

"Wow! What an amazing view! How lucky are you?!" Callie said, walking out to the balcony to take in the breathtaking view of the ocean. She could see God's handy work up close and personal from this vantage point.

"Lucky? At one point, I thought so. Not so much anymore. It costs me... much more than you think," Mercedes said, losing the smile she'd carried on the trip there. "But, hey, everything is a tradeoff, right?"

"I suppose you're right," Callie said.

Feeling the need to change the subject and lighten Mercedes' mood, Callie asked, "What is that amazing smell coming from the kitchen?"

"That's my mommy's recipe for chicken enchiladas," Mercedes responded, renewing her smile. "She taught me how to make it when I was just a little girl. It's one of the few recipes I remember how to make, but I haven't made it since I moved here. You've made me very happy by accepting my invitation, because I got to spend the entire day thinking of my mommy and a time when life was easier."

"I'm honored that I get to share the meal and the memories with you," Callie replied. "I know how much love goes into preparing recipes from loved ones who are no longer able to stand beside us in the kitchen. Every sprinkle of spice brings the flavor of a beautiful memory, and the smile at the end of an empty fork is like a smile from heaven. There's just no greater joy than that, right?"

"Liz, you speak with the tongue of an angel," Mercedes added, her eyes welling up with tears.

Callie walked over and put her arms around Mercedes, giving her a long, but gentle hug, and then wiped a tear from her cheek. Lying to this young woman was becoming more difficult as the days went on, and Callie was finding herself getting more attached. It would take all of her inner strength and a renewed sense of purpose in order to battle her innate instinct to rescue.

"It's got to be margarita time," Callie suggested. "Let's put on some happy music, adjourn to the deck and make fun of attorneys!"

"You're on!" Mercedes quickly agreed.

Girl time went into full swing on the deck, and the enchiladas were just about the most delicious Callie had ever tasted. Mercedes was an amazing culinary artist, and pulled out all the hostess stops, serving them on a beautiful antique ceramic, gold-rimmed platter. The table had been set with plates that matched the platter, dinner napkins, and fine silverware. Callie found herself wishing for a good life for Mercedes. If Operation Duplicity was successful, Callie would do what she could to give her a good start.

A few hours after dinner, and a few more margaritas, Callie got a text. Of course, Mercedes was unaware of it, but it was all part of the next step in Callie's plan to extract the complete truth from Mercedes. Callie had written the text herself from another phone and had set it to be sent to her later in the evening.

As the text notification came through, Callie looked at her phone and changed her smile to a more serious frown. Mercedes noticed, of course, and asked if everything was okay. Callie's web of deceit was working. The spider had caught the unwitting fly.

Callie began to muster up a few tears and with a shaky voice, she said, "My husband's condition has become dire, and they're telling me that if he doesn't have surgery in the next two weeks, he's not going to make it."

Mercedes got up and crossed the room to console her new friend. As she reached over for a hug, Callie began to cry even harder, but threw in words of desperation, stating that she had no idea what she was going to do. Time had run out, and there was no way she would make the $100,000 needed for the surgery in that short amount of time.

Callie looked at Mercedes, tears still streaming from her eyes and said, "I can't live without him. I refuse to let him go because of the lack of money. How can I make this happen? What am I going to do?"

Mercedes was overwhelmed with empathy, which was just enough to get her to take the leap Callie had been waiting for and responded. "I might know of a way, but I'm pretty sure you won't like it because it's not legal, and it's not for a lady such as yourself."

"Mercedes, at this point, there's nothing I wouldn't do for the love of my life. I can't lose him. It would kill me. Please tell me if you know of something I can do to make that kind of money quickly."

Mercedes said, "Let's take some tequila up to the rooftop pool and we can talk about it there. As they sat down at a metal table beside the beautifully lit infinity pool on the roof, Mercedes began to share all of the ugly details of the entirety of her life full of lies in San Jan, the two of them drinking a double shot of Patron tequila.

After having listened to Mercedes' nearly complete confessions for more than 20 minutes, Callie asked, "So you mean a man would pay a hundred grand for one night of sex with a woman?"

Mercedes answered, "That, and more. How do you think I paid for this apartment?"

"So the court reporter job is another lie. How do you pull off that one? That requires a skill and training, especially to secure a realtime job in the federal courts."

"I don't even know. Supposedly, Franco set all of that up with some court reporter who retired and lives somewhere abroad. All of my salary and income from that job goes into a private account for that person. I don't get any of that. I just come to work and pretend to do the job, which is why I don't have anything to do with any of the other reporters in the courthouse. No one up till now has known the truth, except the feds."

"What feds?" Callie asked, interrupting the free-flowing admissions coming from Mercedes. The faucet of confessions had apparently been turned on full blast. Callie was going to take full advantage of it.

"I called my friend I told you about in DC, and she hooked me up with some dude from the FBI. I wanted out of this life, and the only way I could think of was to report Franco and agree to testify in exchange for my immunity. They were supposed to be sending me help. Soon, they said. But I don't think the troops are coming. I wouldn't get you involved in this if the help had actually showed up. But since they're not here and you need the money, this is the quickest way I know to get you what you need."

As soon as Callie heard Mercedes' last statement, although it wasn't quite the plan she had in mind for the evening, she decided it was time to come clean and tell Mercedes who she was. She knew there was a risk that Mercedes would bolt, but if she told her now, it would be better than having the truth come out in the middle of something perhaps more dangerous.

Deciding to ease into it, Callie said, "You know, my young friend, I can't tell you how awful I feel about the tapestry of your life so far. But I'll also tell you how proud I am that you've made a choice that will give you a fresh start at a fulfilling life somewhere else. Very few people have that opportunity, you know? And the fact that you're willing to help someone you barely know tells me so much about who you really are. This is not the role you were meant to play, Mercedes."

Mercedes gave a half smile and said, "Well, thanks, Liz, but I'm not seeing a lot of hope for a fresh start so far."

Callie asked, "Hope is a funny thing. It can come from the least obvious places. Do you believe that?"

"I guess so," Mercedes said as she sighed.

"We've known each other for only a few weeks, but I feel we have a strong bond. Do you agree?"

"I do."

"Okay. I need you to hold onto that trust for the next few minutes. Can you do that?"

"Uh... sure?" Mercedes agreed, but visibly confused, with a resultant crease between her eyebrows.

Callie then broke her cover, at least partially. It would be better for Mercedes if she knew less of the personal details, like

Callie's real name and life story. It was only important that she know that Callie's purpose was to get her that brand-new life she wanted and to do so as not only her FBI confidante, but as her friend. That part wasn't a pretense. It wasn't something Callie had learned to fake, not ever.

Mercedes began to anger when she realized she'd been fooled, but as soon as Callie explained, she began to calm somewhat. Callie reminded her that both had told half lies, and that it was an important part of Callie's mission to secure the truth, which would be hard to ascertain in an FBI capacity. People lie all the time to them, which is the sole reason undercover operations exist.

Mercedes finally said she understood, and Callie began to move forward with the next phase of the plan, which would require Mercedes' help and cooperation. If Mercedes wanted out, it was time to take an active role in ensuring her own, more beautiful future.

"So I'm in your corner," Callie said. "I need for you to be in mine. What do you say the two of us take no prisoners and show Franco just who's really in control?"

As Callie extended her hand to Mercedes, Mercedes refused the hand, but instead reached in for a strong hug and began to sob uncontrollably as she whispered in her ear, "Thank you." These two little words were the catalyst to a brand-new sense of comradery between Callie and Mercedes, and a plan was devised for a good, old-fashioned takedown, with the perfect backdrop of the upcoming baile de màscaras at Franco's private island estate just a few minutes' boat ride from the mainland.

# Chapter 4: Masquerades and Malice

### *Callie's Apartment, January 21...*

The night before with Mercedes had been an emotional rollercoaster for Callie. Thinking back to just three weeks before, she felt as though she was a lifetime away from Austin, her courthouse and her cowboy. It was time to report the successful completion of phase one of Operation Duplicity to Agent Kendrick. She could finally begin to see the light at the end of the proverbial tunnel, and her time in Puerto Rico would be coming to an end soon.

Accessing her secure line, she sat down at the bar and placed the call, opening her field notebook. As she began to share the details of her evening with Mercedes and the plan they'd put in place for the upcoming masquerade ball, Kendrick interrupted.

"Callie, you've done a fine job, but it's time to come home and let the big boys step in. I promised you I wouldn't put you in harm's way, and I'm keeping to that promise. An experienced agent, Carlos Medina, will take it from here. He's been on standby in San Juan, awaiting orders."

"But I've already bonded with Mercedes, and there's no way she's going to trust someone new, especially if it's a man."

"Yes, but it's too dangerous for you to finish the investigation. I'm not willing to risk your safety. If your cover is blown on that island, I only have a limited ability to get you out of there."

Now extremely frustrated, Callie proposed a compromise. What if they made arrangements to get Agent Medina on the guest list? That way, Callie and Mercedes would be protected and could make a quick retreat if there was any sign of trouble.

"In case you hadn't noticed, I can take care of myself," Callie said. "I understand and appreciate your desire to coddle me, and I think I've offered a reasonable compromise, but I need to see this through to the end. I gave my word to Mercedes, and I always keep my word."

Agent Kendrick must have been mulling things over, because he was silent for more than just a few seconds, prompting Callie to ask if he was still on the line.

"Yes, I'm here, Callie. I'm just weighing the risks and potential outcomes. If something happens to you, I'd not only have to explain to my superiors, but also to Dominic and your family. That puts me in a difficult position."

"Noted," followed Callie, "but let's consider why you called me in the first place. Any field agent could have done this mission, with the proper amount of research. You must have seen some value in choosing me instead. I aced every physical and mental test you put me through in training. Have I not proven my value in the field?"

"You have a valid point, Callie. You missed your calling. You should have been a negotiator," Kendrick said, chuckling.

"Ha ha. I was born that way. Just ask my family. So does that mean I'm staying?" Callie asked.

"Just through the masquerade ball. I'll get Medina on the list and follow up with the final details tomorrow. Your only task will be to place a listening device in a discreet location in the estate. Get in, and get out. No horsing around. Do you understand? The slightest hint of trouble, and you're to abort the mission."

Callie began to smile again, feeling accomplished, and responded, "Agreed. Thank you, Kendrick! You won't be sorry."

Bringing the call to a close, she tossed the phone on the sofa, opened a cold Corona and toasted to the heavens, shouting, "Did you hear that, Daddy? I've still got it."

The masquerade ball would be just six days from now. Callie and Mercedes had arranged to get together on Thursday evening so that Callie could try on gowns and heels. Not surprisingly, Mercedes had a closetful of designer gowns from which to choose. Friday would be spent indulging in mani-pedis, hair, makeup and, of course, shopping for the appropriate masks to wear.

Three days in court went by at a snail's pace, it seemed, but Thursday finally arrived, and court was closed for the rest of the week due to some much-needed security upgrades to the courthouse. Callie tried to sleep in, but it just wasn't possible, so she decided to take a short walk on the beach. She hadn't been in her car since she'd been shopping at the mall, but traffic wouldn't be bad in the middle of the day during a workweek.

Hitting the white sands of Condado Beach, Callie slipped out of her coverall and walked down to the water's edge, dipping her toes into the mud. Feeling the wet sand squish between her toes, she was reminded of her childhood visits to her aunt and uncle's home down the street.

She'd made the mistake, only once, of leaving her shoes outside their front door. Always the pranksters, you never knew what to expect while you were with this loving couple. This particular memory involved Callie's toes being greeted by peanut butter which had been spooned into the front of her favorite sneakers. It was such a gross feeling at the time, but a memory that had brought so much laughter over the course of Callie's life, including this very minute.

After a walk on the beach, Callie took a refreshing swim in the ocean. The water was so clear here that she could see straight through to the bottom, which was a good thing. Callie had a closeted, but deep-rooted fear of water. It was something she'd forced herself to overcome, but anything bigger than a swimming pool brought it back up to the surface. So anything past waist deep was out of the question in the ocean.

Callie knew the exact origin of this fear. It arose, as many fears do, out of a childhood trauma. At the tender age of four, she was on a summer visit with her aunt in Columbus, Mississippi, and they took the ski boat out on Lake Lowndes. In the middle of the lake, the outboard motor had become dislodged. Callie's aunt turned off the motor, jumped into the water and attempted to lift it back into its slot, but her swimsuit bottom got caught in the blades of the propeller.

At this point, Callie, sitting in the middle of the boat with her orange lifejacket securely fastened, heard her aunt say, "Callie, call for help!" Although she'd tried, she was so terrified that her tiny, trembling voice could only whisper. The weight of the heavy motor was pulling her aunt under, and Callie began to cry.

Luckily, a passing double-decker boat came cruising nearby and noticed this little girl sitting mysteriously by herself and rushed into rescue mode. For Callie, however, the trauma of that event created her aquaphobia, which stayed with her through adulthood. She would never allow herself to be in a body of water that left her feeling helpless.

Today, however, Callie was feeling exhilarated and proud of her undercover savvy, as if she could conquer any fear. It was just great exercise in the beautiful blue-green saltwater. But after about half an hour, it was time for Callie to shower off the salt and get back to the apartment. Mercedes would be picking her up at around 5:00 for an early dinner and cocktails at a local pub, followed by a little closet shopping for the perfect gown.

Most of the afternoon was spent making notes to discuss with Mercedes about their plan for getting the listening device placed at Franco's estate. From what Callie had gathered from her conversation with Mercedes, she'd been there numerous times, and she knew the layout. That meant she should be able to pinpoint the perfect location for the bug, and they could be in and out without notice.

Once the notes were down on paper, Callie decided to bake a batch of her favorite brownies to share with Mercedes later in the evening. At about 4:00, though, she found herself in need of one of those with an afternoon jolt of caffeine. *Ahh... complete satisfaction*, Callie thought, taking the first mouth-watering bite of chocolatey heaven.

Mercedes soon was knocking at the door, and the two were off to dinner and drinks. Patrick's Irish Pub was truly fantastic! The beer-battered fish was the best Callie had ever tasted, and the fries were pure genius. They were dipped in the same batter and deep fried with the fish. Easy on the palate, for sure, but there was so much food that Callie and Mercedes opted to share a plate.

After paying the dinner tab, they moved outside and ordered a couple of Long Island Iced Teas, toasting to their final few days in San Juan.

The moon was now casting its golden glow over the ocean view from the deck of Patrick's, and Mercedes suggested they get started back to her apartment. Preparing for a late night and their early morning appointment at the spa, Callie had accepted Mercedes' invitation to stay the night. Mercedes would just drop her off after their day of pampering and shopping for masks.

As soon as they walked in the door, Callie put the brownies on the counter and said, "A treat for later," and followed Mercedes into her spare bedroom, which she had turned into a closet. On one wall, there were shoes on shelves from floor to ceiling, with a ladder that was attached inside a track at the ceiling, allowing it to move along the wall and lock into place. This was a shoe collection that could give Imelda Marcos a run for her money.

On the opposite wall, there, in all their splendor, hung gowns, with sequins and satin and lace everywhere. Every color in the rainbow was represented, and then some. Callie attempted to go through them, but clearly was overwhelmed. It was at that point that Mercedes began to pull out a few that she thought would be perfect for Callie.

After two hours of trying on gown upon gown, the perfect one fell into her hands and then onto her body. Although Callie had always detested trying on clothes in a store, when she'd tried on something that worked, she just felt it. And this dress seemed to have been made for her, just like the one Dom had gotten her for the Christmas party, except much more formal.

The color was gold, but not just any gold. The fabric was silk, and because of its slink factor and the way it flowed on Callie's body, it appeared as if she was wearing liquid gold, poured from a freshly melted gold bar. Sleeveless, but high at the neck with a drawstring closure, it would be the perfect backdrop for the spy necklace that Dom had given her.

Mercedes chose a red gown adorned with white glittery lace around the sweeping neckline and around the generous slit in the front. They would be the bells of the ball, in disguise along with everyone else at the party, but in a way that no one else would be; the truest definition of hiding in plain sight.

In their conversation over wardrobe selections, Mercedes told Callie that Franco seemed to be excited when she told him of another desperate, gorgeous woman she'd be bringing as her guest for the evening. He clearly had no idea that his entire life would come crashing down around him very soon.

After bagging Callie's gown and shoes up, the two went into the kitchen to grab a few bottles of water and the brownies to take up to the rooftop pool. It was time to finalize their plan and talk about the details of what each of them would do once arriving at the estate.

Mercedes said that Franco's private study was her pick of the most ideal location for the listening device. It was where he did all of his unsavory business, and with few exceptions, no one was allowed inside; not the staff, and certainly not his wife. She'd only seen it a few times herself, and she was his most trusted lady in that aspect of the business.

The study was up the stairs on the second level, to the rear of the estate, behind a second set of double doors which could only be opened with a passkey. Luckily, Mercedes had watched as Franco entered it while in a drunken stupor at a party more than a year ago. She somehow knew it might be a good thing to memorize, and she'd had it in her head the entire time. The code of 8675309 brought laughter to them both as Mercedes recited it to Callie.

"Are you kidding me?" Callie said, attempting to control her laughter.

"No. How do you think I remembered it so easily?" Mercedes said, joining in the laughter.

And with that, they moved on to Mercedes' part in the mission. She would simply be the decoy. She was going to distract the guard standing at the end of the hallway. He was always there during parties, and coincidentally, he was always hitting on Mercedes. She'd only have to wink his way and he'd be a goner.

In the event something went awry, Callie let Mercedes know that they had backup. Agent Medina would be in attendance somewhere. She'd get the final details on his exact position from Kendrick on Saturday morning. Mercedes was happy that Callie had insisted on staying through to the end. As Callie had already discerned, Mercedes didn't trust any man at this point in the game.

With the roles laid out and the brownie pan completely empty, Callie and Mercedes went back downstairs to get some sleep. Mercedes made up the sofa for Callie, with fluffy pillows and a soft comforter, and retreated to her bedroom for the night. The day had been long, but productive, and Callie was asleep in no time.

Morning coffee and the sunlight greeted Callie, and she got up to take one last look at the glorious view from Mercedes' balcony. This would be the last time she would be here, which made her a little sad, but as she stepped outside and felt the ocean mist and the warmth of the sun on her cheeks, she had a sense of pride in herself and the work she'd done. And this led to a vision of her homecoming celebration with Dom. She couldn't wait to get back home. The girl could leave the country, but the country would never leave the girl.

The spa was a once-in-a-lifetime experience with Mercedes. They really rolled out the red carpet and gave Callie and Mercedes the royal treatment. They were eating delicacies and drinking mimosas while getting foot rubs and nails painted over the course of four unbelievable hours. It was quite an extravagant and unforgettable morning, but the day wasn't over yet. Eventually, it was time to head over to Old San Juan for the perfect masquerade.

The tiny, colorful shops in Old San Juan lined the narrow, brick-paved streets which made it difficult to walk in heels. Thankfully, this wasn't a work day, and Callie and Mercedes having just had a pedicure, were already wearing flip-flops. When they entered the costume store, they saw it was filled to the brim with costumes and masks to fit any budget and heart's desire, but in just a few seconds, Callie had already spotted the one she wanted hanging on the wall behind the counter.

Coincidentally, Mercedes was looking in the same direction and found one hanging right next to the one Callie had asked the clerk to retrieve for her. Callie's was multiple shades of red, with sparkly swirls in the center of the nose and around the eyes. It would not only complement her gown, but it was also the perfect match for her spycam ruby necklace. The mask Mercedes chose was stark white with glittery white lace.

Now that the ensemble was complete, Callie was ready to return to her apartment, make more notes and call it an early night. They agreed to meet at the ferry slip the following afternoon at 5:00 p.m. Twenty minutes after that, they would be off onto the water.

Callie fell asleep with the pen in her hand while lying on the sofa and awoke around 3:00 a.m. to a light rain tapping on the metal table on the balcony. She got up and turned on the outside light, thinking to herself that rain wouldn't be a welcome friend while wearing a gown aboard a local ferry. "Go away until the party is over!" she said, as if that had ever worked.

Realizing that the weather was above her paygrade, she got into bed and slept in a little longer, this time awakening to the sound of her FBI-issued phone. It was a quick update call between herself and Kendrick. He let her know that Agent Medina would be working as a server at the ball. He'd make contact with her by bringing her a drink and asking her if she preferred white or red, and she'd respond by telling him she preferred rich.

Callie, in turn, gave Kendrick the details of where the listening device would be planted, and assured him that she and Mercedes had everything under control and would take no unnecessary risks, at which point she hung up, put her robe on and went for her first cup of coffee.

As she looked out the window, it was a perfectly clear day. She was grateful that it appeared her wish had been granted and the rain was simply a passing sprinkle to cool things off a bit. It was going to be a lazy day, her last one in San Juan, and in just 24 hours, she'd be back in the strong and loving arms of her cowboy.

The hours ticked away as Callie lounged on the couch, praying for the strength and courage to complete the tasks she'd been assigned in the safest and most expeditious manner possible. She had achieved many things in her life, the most important of which was the birth of her two beautiful, happy and healthy children. No achievement would ever be as important as that one.

This endeavor felt as if it were a close second, though. Callie's country was depending on her to ensure that justice prevailed. This young woman was depending on her to carry her forward into a new life. And the people she loved were depending on her to return home safely to them. This was one of those character builders her dad had always coached her about, and she wasn't taking it lightly.

The clock began to chime at 3:00, and it was time to get showered, dressed, armed and out the door. She'd be wearing the thigh holster and pistol Dom had given her beneath her golden gown, and the recording device would be hidden inside her cellphone. She'd already assumed security would be checking purses, but not suspecting a woman to be wearing a weapon. And her gown, although full length in the back, fell just below the knee in the front, so there was plenty of room to reach in and grab it if necessary.

At around 4:00, Callie made her way into the bedroom and began to get ready. Shower complete in her usual half hour, she reached into that beautiful red box, pulled out the necklace, pushed the back of the ruby and fastened it securely around her neck. All of a sudden, she felt Dom and began to talk to him as if he were standing beside her. She shared with him her progress so far and the details of the night, letting him know she'd be home the next day.

Hearing the cab driver honk for her downstairs, she grabbed her red sequined bag, saying, "Babe, if you can hear me, I love you. Wish me luck!" Upon arrival at the ferry slip, she spotted Mercedes' red gown almost immediately and walked over to wait with her for the ferry to arrive. As scheduled, they promptly departed for the island estate at 5:20. The waters seemed a little choppy on the ride over, but it was a ten-minute trip, for which Callie was extremely grateful.

The ferry slowly edged its way up to the dock at the base of the island, and Callie mused that it looked more mountainous than she had imagined it. The estate couldn't even be seen from the dock. There appeared to be only beach and trees and rocky cliffs, giving it the feel of a place from which someone would want to be rescued. Mercedes noticed the look of concern on Callie's face and told her that Franco specifically bought this island because it was well hidden and protected, much like a fortress. Given his web of secrets and the types of people who visited the island, it all made perfect sense.

Disembarking the ferry along with about 20 other guests, they made their way up the wood-planked deck and walked up a few brick steps, where, again to Callie's surprise, several Hummer limos were all lined up and waiting, complete with uniformed chauffeurs standing at attention, hats in hand. Callie and Mercedes took the first in line, and Callie couldn't help thinking to herself that she'd never taken quite this many modes of transportation to arrive at a party. It was going to be a night to remember, for sure!

The winding paved road up to the estate was a sight like none other. The cliffs on one side stretched as far as the eye could see, but the freshly planted flowers and tropical bushes nestled into the indigenous trees reminded Callie of the many botanical gardens she's visited in the South.

As they rounded the final curve and the road straightened out, the most enormous estate Callie had ever seen appeared in the distance. This place was one for the memory books. It mirrored a large castle in size, but its architecture was clearly Mediterranean in style. Stucco siding, a red tiled rooftop, and ornate wrought-iron handrails and window accents adorned this massive estate. It was lit up and decorated for the evening, and security was out in full force, checking invitations and purses at the grand front entryway.

Security waved Callie and Mercedes through the front door as if they belonged there. Mercedes then winked at Callie as if to say, *I have friends in high places*, nodding her head in the direction of the stairway to Franco's study. Within seconds, they were greeted by their hosts, Franco and his wife, Ingrid. She was a 50-ish, stunning, blonde bombshell, with emerald green eyes glimmering through her pewter mask.

"Welcome to our home," Ingrid said, extending her hand.

As Callie extended her hand in kind, thanking her for the invitation, Ingrid enveloped Callie's hand into both of hers. Callie then shifted her eyes to Franco, because she could see the uncomfortable, undressing of his eyes in her periphery. Caught off guard, he moved his eyes to her eyes and said, "Yes, welcome. Please, make yourselves comfortable. An evening of intrigue awaits you." And then, as Ingrid turned to greet another guest, Franco whispered to them, "8:00 p.m., blue lanai," and quickly joined Ingrid.

Callie remarked to Mercedes how sorry she felt for Ingrid. If she knew what her husband was involved in, she'd probably be devastated. Mercedes followed the remark with what she'd been told by Franco about her; that she was always traveling and wasn't concerned with what he did or with whom.

"She didn't seem to me to be exactly a cold fish." Callie said. "Did you see the way she gently welcomed me? I got a warm, fuzzy feeling from her."

Mercedes responded, "I saw that. I've met her a few times, and she never gave me that feeling, but maybe she knows more than he thinks, and she just turns a blind eye to it."

"That's possible, I guess. After we leave here, she won't be able to do that for much longer."

"Yes. She'll be saying good-bye to this life, just like I will. The only difference is that everyone will know who she is, and I get to go off the radar. That does make me feel a little sorry for her."

Thinking it may be time for a glass of wine and a nibble of something to eat, the two stepped further into the room where the band was just setting up and the trays were being loaded with culinary delights. Almost as if on cue, a server approached them with a tray of filled wine glasses.

"Do you prefer white or red?" he asked?

And exactly as she'd been told, this was her contact, Agent Medina. And boy, was he a welcome sight! An early contact by an experienced agent gave Callie an extra sense of security, and she quickly responded with, "I prefer rich." The three of them laughed, as Callie took a glass of white, Mercedes opting for a glass of red, the two of them nodding a much more meaningful thank-you than usual.

The room was beginning to fill up with masked-adorned guests, and the band was doing their sound check. Once the music began to play and people were occupied with eating, drinking and being merry, that's when Callie and Mercedes quietly made their way past Agent Medina, who was standing in the doorway of the ballroom. As they passed him, he nodded to indicate that the coast was clear.

No one was anywhere near the front stairway, so the two made their way to the top of the stairs. The first room on that wing of the hallway was a guest bath. Mercedes said to Callie, "Wait inside here and give me five minutes. I'll knock on the door when it's time."

"Okay. Be careful, Mercedes."

"Piece of cake, Liz. Big muscular men turn into wimpy little boys with the fluttering of these eyelashes. You need to be in and out of the study in two minutes, though. I'm not planning on giving up the gold for this one."

"Done. I'll knock on the bathroom door on my way downstairs, and you can pretend that you'll meet him later."

Five minutes later, there was the knock on the bathroom door, and Callie came out and walked briskly back through the double doors to the study. Entering the code of 8675309 on the security panel, the beep sounded and the door automatically opened. Callie had already retrieved the SIM card from her phone while she was waiting in the bathroom, but she was going to locate the cellphone that Franco used for his secret business.

She opened every drawer in the desk in a hurried fashion, and finally found it just inside the lap drawer. She quickly inserted the SIM card into the phone, put it back in its exact location in the drawer and left the room. As she did, she heard a boom of thunder outside that shook her in her heels. Quickly regaining her composure, she rushed back down the hall and knocked on the door to the bathroom, signaling to Mercedes to come out.

When she got to the bottom of the stairs, she heard Mercedes giggle a bit and looked up to see her kissing the burly guard and slowly descending the stairs. Mission accomplished, it was time to join the rest of the guests at the party, mingle a little, and get a necessary shot of tequila to calm their very frazzled nerves. They would also need to follow through with meeting Franco on the blue lanai, so as not to create any sort of suspicion on his part. They had an hour, though, and decided to spend it enjoying themselves. They separated and each took a corner of the room, agreeing to meet at the double doors to the rear of the ballroom, which opened to the patio. From there, they'd walk down the steps and around the outer walkway to the blue lanai and meet with Franco, after which they'd get in the limo and Operation Duplicity would be trail dust.

Callie walked up and introduced herself to a young couple, but before she could get her entire name out, another loud clap of thunder, accompanied by several flashes of lightening, shook the walls of the estate. It was more than clear that the storm was no longer in the distance. She desperately wanted to get back home before the storm blew in, because even a short ferry ride in a tropical storm wouldn't do at all. There was no amount of alcohol that could conquer her aquaphobia, and she could feel it swelling up inside.

Needing reassurance, she looked for Mercedes and Agent Medina. She spotted Mercedes deep in conversation with a tall man across the room, and Agent Medina was nearby, still holding his tray of wine. Almost as soon as her pulse began to return to its normal rate, the lights began to flicker, and then... complete darkness.

The silence in the room was deafening, as the band stopped playing. And without an opportunity to adjust her vision to the darkness, Callie felt a hand over her mouth and strong arms around her, lifting her feet off the ground and removing her to parts unknown. *Oh, my God! Oh, my God! What's happening?!* she thought.

As the generator kicked in and the lights returned, Callie found herself behind a locked metal door. She could smell the ocean nearby, and she could hear the wind howling, but she had no clue where she was. She began to call out loudly for help, but through the metal door, she heard the sound of Mercedes' voice.

"Liz, is that you? Are you okay?"

"Yes. Mercedes? Are you okay? What happened? Where are we?"

"I'm okay. I'm not sure where we are, but I think we're in the underground storm shelter. I've never seen it, but Franco told me he had one built."

A storm shelter in an estate on a tropical island was a great idea, but why would the doors lock from the outside? And why would there be more than one? Regardless of the why, it was time to find a way out. This wasn't Callie's plan. She wanted her cowboy more than ever now. And that thought reminded her of her spycam necklace.

"Dom, if you can hear me, I'm in trouble. I'm somewhere under this godforsaken island in the middle of a storm, and I really need my cowboy." Callie said desperately. Almost immediately, she thought about the ridiculousness of her pleas for Dom to rescue her. He was on the ranch in Austin, and there was no way to tell if he'd even see this so that he could send help. She had the tracking device in her purse, but would it work so that Kendrick would see her exact location if she was underground? She wasn't sure where Agent Medina was, but he couldn't have foreseen any of this. Maybe he could find them.

Deep in quiet thought, Callie heard the unfamiliar voice of another woman... and then another... and another. There were at least three other women in the same location with her and Mercedes, all locked behind metal doors. None of them had any idea where they were, but they'd all been guests at the ball.

Something more sinister was going on here. Of that, Callie was certain. Needless to say, things were looking bleak, and all of a sudden, the squeaking sound of the slamming of a metal door and nearing footsteps could be heard. Callie's pulse began to race as the footsteps came closer, the lock on the door ticked, and the door flung open. It was Franco, and he was armed.

Callie reached for her thigh-holstered weapon, and Franco said, "I wouldn't," and ordered his burly goon to take it from her. "So you thought you were smart enough to take me down? Admittedly, you had a nice plan, and you were good enough to get my best girl to help you with it, but there was one tiny, unplanned glitch. Mercedes didn't know about the silent alarm and hidden camera I had installed in my study last week. And now I have to decide what to do with you two. You see, I'm not going to jail, and you're not going to tell anybody anything. As luck would have it, some of my guests here tonight were invited for the explicit purpose of purchasing commodities; the beautiful kind. I think you both will bring a very high price, don't you?"

"Women are NOT commodities, you disgusting little man. There's no way you're going to sell us like pieces of furniture," Callie responded.

And then suddenly, the henchman dropped to the ground, causing Franco to turn his back on Callie, and in a split second, he was disarmed and in the clutches of a chokehold. It had all happened so quickly, and the room was so dimly lit that Callie was trying to wrap her mind around what had just happened. And then she heard the deep, raspy voice she knew so well. "I couldn't have said it better myself, Darlin'." It was Dom. But how?

"Oh, my God! Dom! You're here!" Callie said, with the sound of relief and complete joy in her voice.

"You said you needed me, right? So where else would I be? Check his pockets for the key to the doors and get everybody out."

Callie reached into Franco's jacket pocket, found the key and unlocked the doors, and then Dom had Callie and Mercedes zip-tie Franco and his goon to a metal pole support structure in the room. Once the two men were securely fettered, Callie grabbed Dom and hugged him tighter than she ever had, kissing him gently on the lips. She couldn't resist her need to know how he'd gotten there so quickly.

He explained that he couldn't quite come to terms with their previous agreement over this mission. Although he was supportive of her desire to do it, there was no way he could risk losing her. In light of that, he had arrived in San Juan the week before, after checking on her progress with Kendrick, and through his own connections, had gotten himself an invitation to the ball.

Mercedes jokingly interrupted and asked, "So you two know each other, I guess?"

"Something like that." Callie said, hugging Dom again.

"I wondered why he was asking so many questions when we were talking earlier," Mercedes remarked.

"Oh, my gosh! So that was the tall, masked man I saw you with just before the lights went out."

"Yes, that's him. And here, I thought he was interested in me."

"Not going to happen, girlfriend. Every step I took in my life got me to this one, but your cowboy is out there somewhere. We just need to get out of here." Callie said.

And just as Dom reached down to hug Callie once more before planning their exit strategy, she felt a jar to her body, as Dom fell to the ground. She looked down and called his name, but looked up again to see Ingrid, with a gun aimed directly in her face. Shocked and not really understanding what just happened, she looked down at Dom again, as the blood began to seep out of the wound on his head.

"Don't worry, silly girl. I didn't kill him. He'll just be out until we're long gone."

"Ingrid, what's going on? Why did you do that? He's the good guy. Franco is the criminal," Callie said, as she kneeled down to check Dom's pulse. He was still alive, thank God. But Callie was really confused about this new piece of the puzzle.

"You think Franco is in charge?" Ingrid said. "Of course, you would. Most women view themselves as the pawns on some man's chess board. Well, not me. I'm in charge. Franco is a weak little man who does what I tell him to do. I have the board, and all the pieces are mine to move about as I see fit."

Callie had seriously misread Ingrid. Mercedes clearly had a better read on her. This was where street smarts won out over classroom training, and maybe even field experience. To beat a criminal, you really needed to think like one; that was something Callie hadn't learned quite yet.

With Dom on the floor and a gun on in her face, the options seemed to be limited for Callie and the group of ladies. And things got worse as Ingrid ordered her group of guards to untie Franco and take the girls to the boat. Escorted by an armed guard down the dimly lit, stone-lined hallway, Callie began to hear the sound of boats rocking on the water. Within a hundred yards, she was surprised to see an underground boat dock that had apparently been cut into the mountainside.

There were two cabin-cruisers sitting side by side moored to the dock, and the ladies were ordered onto one of them. Callie's worst nightmare was happening right before her eyes. She had no clue where they were taking her, but at this point, it didn't matter. The love of her life was injured, and she was being forced to leave him behind, on a boat, in the middle of an angry storm.

Franco stayed behind as Ingrid and the rest of the crew joined the ladies. Callie and Mercedes were holding hands and saying their prayers together, but Ingrid told them that God wasn't listening to them. Callie couldn't resist a response and said, "You apparently don't know God, because he always listens. He's watching right now."

Oh, yeah? Well, He's not the one with the gun, is He?" Ingrid said.

"No, but the power of God will always overpower anything in your arsenal," said Mercedes. "You only think you're in charge."

As the boat moved from the shelter of the island caverns into the fierce tropical storm, it was tossed from wave to wave as if it were a child's toy. The sea was angry, and Callie's fears of both the water and her current predicament quickly brought her into a warrior state of mind. Though Mercedes grabbed her hand and tried to stop her, she lunged towards Ingrid and struggled for the gun.

Mercedes looked to the rear of the boat, and in the distance, could see another boat with Dom and Agent Medina speeding up to them. She shouted to Callie, "Liz, stop! Dom's coming!" Callie turned to look, and as she did, Ingrid hit her in the back of the head with the gun, and she was tossed overboard, drifting into the abyss of the now darkened ocean. The only sign of her was the floating red mask that had once covered her face.

As Callie began to sink and slowly lose consciousness, she tried to stay in control, but she couldn't fight the strong current. Her eyelids began to close, and flashes of memories came flooding across her mind's eye. First, her lovely grandma, her gentle and kindhearted dad; then her loving husband, Mike, the two beautiful children that they had raised, and her grandchildren, Michael and Sophia.

And then, as her body gave way to the ocean's power, there was one sweet, but fleeting thought of Dom. She would never see him again. She would miss all the special moments she'd been looking forward to with her family. Was this God's plan? Was she going to die at the hands of the ocean; something she had feared for the majority of her life?

As Callie's body went cold, there was complete silence. She was simply following the directions of the ocean now. If this was the plan, she had no control over it.

## Chapter 5:  Friends in High Places

*Three days later...*

Groggily awaking from her unconscious state, Callie opened her eyes in a confused state.  Through her blurry eyes, she strained to see the figure of an elderly, gray and balding man smiling and gazing at her with the sweetest blue eyes.  Her voice still shaky and her throat dry, she quietly asked, "Daddy?"

"Welcome back, young lady.  I'm somebody's daddy, but not yours.  My name is Dr. Thomas Forsythe, but you can call me Tom.  I thought you were a goner when I found you on the beach.  You barely had a pulse, but luckily, I had everything I needed here to take care of you."

"Tom?  That was my daddy's name.  Thank you so much for taking care of me."

With a quick check of her vitals, Dr. Forsythe asked, "Can you tell me your name?"

"Liz — I mean, Callie."

"Well, those are so far apart.  Which one is it?"

"It's both, actually, but you can call me Callie."

"When I found you, you had on a formal gown.  There has to be a story there."

"Yes, there is, but the details are fuzzy at the moment."

"Of course, they are. How about I get you some water and we stop those fluids I'm running through your veins? The details will come in time, and we can call your family. I'm sure they're looking for you."

He walked out of the room briefly, and came back in with a glass of water and a straw, offering it to Callie. He then showed her the necklace he'd put in a cloth-covered box on the counter.

"You were wearing this beautiful necklace too. It's obviously one of a kind. Does it ring any bells for you?"

"Dom," Callie answered quietly.

"Dom? Is that a code word for something?"

"No," Callie said, giving him a grin. "It's short for Dominic. He's my boyfriend. I have to call him. He must be frantic about now."

Tom got his phone and dialed the number Callie gave him and handed her the phone. When Dom answered, Callie, still a little hoarse and weak, simply said his name, and he began to sob uncontrollably.

"I'm okay, Babe. It's all going to be fine."

"Callie, I thought I'd lost you. We've been searching the ocean and up and down the shoreline for days! Where are you?"

"I'm not sure, but this kind doctor, Dr. Forsythe, found me on a beach somewhere and has been taking care of me. I'm going to hand him the phone and he can tell you exactly how to get here. I love you, Dom."

"I love you too, Callie. I'll see you as soon as possible."

The doctor gave Dom the directions to his place on a tiny island just across the bay from Franco's estate. It was an easy boat ride from San Juan, but Dom was in such a hurry to get to her that he flew the FBI copter instead. The doctor had a helipad on the grounds because of his medical travels to and from the States.

In just 20 minutes, she heard the doorbell, and then his lovely voice as Tom greeted him. Her mind wanted her to race into his arms, but her body wouldn't allow it. So this time, she waited for the few seconds it took him to get to her side and hug and kiss her, running his soft and gentle hands through her hair.

"I must look horrible," Callie said.

"Really? Darlin', even at your worst, you put every other woman to shame. Your beautiful eyes and smile make vision worth having."

"Always the charmer, right, Cowboy?"

"Just an honest man, Callie."

Tom walked back into the room to check Callie's vitals again, and Dom stood up to shake his hand and tell him the debt of gratitude he owed him for saving Callie's life.

"If there's ever anything in the world I can do for you, you just name it. I'll never be able to repay your kindness in watching over my lady, but I can give it my best shot."

Tom paused for a second, something sad coming to his eyes. "I lost someone about three years ago," he said. "I'm not sure if she's still living, but she disappeared suddenly. So I know how it feels to have your heart ripped out. I can't tell you how happy I was that I could get Callie back in your arms. I wish someone could have done that for me."

Callie, listening as the two were talking, interrupted and asked the doctor for details. He began to explain that it was his 30-year-old daughter, Samantha, and that she had disappeared while visiting a girlfriend in San Juan. The last communication he'd had from her was that she and her friend had been invited to a masquerade ball on a private island.

He'd moved to San Juan shortly after it became clear that the authorities would be of no help, but had come up empty-handed except for his personal observation that the private island across the way seemed to be having lots of those types of parties. He'd seen many young women being transported on and off the island, but couldn't get close enough to get any further details.

After sharing his story, Tom suggested that they let Callie rest. Dom agreed, giving her a final kiss and assuring her he'd be right outside the room. He whispered in her ear, "I know what you're thinking, Darlin', but you get some rest and we'll talk later."

Callie wanted to help Tom, and she knew that Dom picked up on that. Right now, however, she wasn't in a position to offer much. She knew she had to recuperate, both physically and mentally, but the time would come when she would reach out to Tom, no matter what. He had given her a second chance at life and continued love, and she wanted to do the same for him.

Hours later, as darkness set in on the shores of Tom's tiny island home, Callie awakened to find Dom sitting in the chair beside her bed. As the two began to talk, Dom filled in the gaps since Callie's fall into the ocean. Callie listened intently while he recounted every minute.

Dom had been pursuing the boat and watched as Callie's body went sailing overboard, and Agent Medina took the wheel as Dom jumped into the waters in an attempt to find her. Medina had continued pursuit of Ingrid and the other ladies, and watched as she ordered every lady to jump into the water. She must have known that Medina would stop to rescue the ladies, and she was right.

Medina circled and fished all the ladies out of the water, and Ingrid and her crew had escaped... for now. Dom assured Callie that the authorities would eventually catch up to them. INTERPOL was already on the case.

With the ladies safely inside the boat, Medina returned to aid Dom in his search for Callie, but insisted that he get back into the boat because the current was too strong. Dom made several more attempts to dive deeper, each time to no avail. And while he wasn't about to give up, he knew it would be easier to bring in the search and rescue team, with the storm moving through and beginning to clear within the next few minutes.

As for Mercedes, she'd been in tears over Callie's disappearance, but was handed over to Agent Kendrick for processing, and arrangements were being made for her departure under the witness protection program the following morning. She proved to be a very valuable asset to the feds, and as a result, several arrests were made.

Along with his henchmen, Franco was arrested at his estate, and all of his assets were immediately frozen. He was already on his way to Washington, courtesy of the U.S. Marshals Service, and he would be standing before a federal judge in the United States in the coming weeks.

"Callie, I'm so proud of you. You have served your country well. A month ago, you were quietly listening to testimony from criminal investigators, and relatively soon, your investigation will be presented on the witness stand by Agent Kendrick. I always knew you were a little Texas tornado, but Washington knows it now."

"Thanks, Babe. I hadn't thought of it quite like that, but that's probably because at the moment, I feel like I've been hit by a Texas tornado," Callie said, laughing and then wincing a bit. "I want to see Mercedes off before she leaves in the morning. Can we make that happen?"

"I'll make the arrangements, Darlin'. I know I couldn't talk you out of it anyway."

"You know me well. And while I'm making requests, I want to help Tom find his daughter."

Dom's smile changed to a look of serious concern, but he said, "Well, I sort of thought that's where your head would be. I saw the look in your eyes when he was telling his story. I hope you understand my concern after what just happened. I'm just not willing to let you out of my sight again. I —"

Callie quickly interjected, "But Dom..."

"Wait, Callie. Let me finish. What I was going to say is that I know how important this is to you, and it's equally important to me. So what do you say we do this one together? I can leave the ranch for this kind of project. It's not super busy right now."

"Oh, Dom! Really!? The two of us together on a mission?"

"Aren't we already on a joint mission? It's sort of a perfect next step, right?"

"This is one the reasons I love you so much," Callie said. "Let's seal the deal with a kiss."

"Hold your horses, missy. I have one condition."

"What is it?"

"We have to go home first. You have to get back to a hundred percent before you go out again. You also need to see the kids. And while you're convalescing, we can start to gather some more intel. Once we get that together, we can give Tom a call and offer to help. Until then, we can't talk to him about this. That's the deal. If you agree to my conditions, then the kiss is forthcoming."

"Deal! Now, bring yourself over here, Cowboy." And he did, and got into the bed to snuggle up for a little while.

Tom had made a pot roast for dinner, and it was so amazing that Callie asked for the recipe. Thrilled that she loved it enough to ask, he happily gave it to her. With a full stomach and Dom watching over her, Callie slept more soundly than she had since she left home.

Anxious to see Mercedes, Callie woke up early the next morning. She was feeling a little stronger, but after they'd said their good-byes and thanked Tom again, Dom insisted on wheeling her out to the copter. It was a short flight to the airport, but Dom was in full caretaker mode at the moment, and Callie was letting him enjoy that.

The copter landed just outside one of the private hangars at the airport in San Juan, where Mercedes was eagerly awaiting Callie's arrival. Dom lifted her out and onto the pavement, and Mercedes ran over to them with open arms and screaming, "Liz!"

Callie greeted her with a warm hug and said, "I'm so happy to see you, Mercedes! Look what we did!! Your new life is just hours away, and I got a second chance to continue mine! I guess we both have friends in high places."

Mercedes was grinning from ear to ear. All of the stress seemed to have faded from this young woman's beautiful eyes, which filled Callie's heart with such pride and joy. What a gift she'd been given, to be able to be a part of something bigger than herself and her family. The last 30 days of Callie's journey, up to and including her resultant near-death experience, were worth every risk she'd taken and everything she'd given up... just to get to this one moment.

Kendrick came up and shook Callie's hand, commending her for a job well done and thanking her on behalf of the President for her service to her country. He told Mercedes it was time to go, but before she did, she wanted to say something else to Callie.

"Although I don't know your true name, wherever I go, I will remember you as my best friend. Because of you, I get to have my pot at the end of the rainbow, and maybe my own cowboy someday."

Callie, with tears in her eyes, said, "That's because of you. Sometimes we just need someone to stand behind us, forcing us to stand still and look in the mirror long enough to see all the value we truly have to offer the world. That was all I did. Now go get your dreams."

The two hugged one last time, and Mercedes turned, not looking back, and boarded the Learjet for parts unknown. Callie and Dom watched until it turned into a tiny dot in the sky, and then Dom asked, "Ready to saddle up our own winged, silver steed?"

"I'd love to, but I still have to pack my things."

"Already done, Darlin'. I had someone pack your things last night, when I was making the call to charter a private jet home.

"Of course you did. I forgot who I was dealing with."

"So it seems." Dom said, giving Callie his very sexy wink.

"Then what are we waiting for? Take me back to Texas, Cowboy."

As they boarded the jet and the wheels left the pavement, Callie looked out the window to the majestic beauty of the island. And then she turned her eyes toward this beautiful man sitting beside her and thought to herself, *Home... it never looked so good.*